LOVE
AND OTHER STORIES

# LOVE
# AND OTHER STORIES

*Mary Mannion*

*First published Nov 2021*

ISBN 978-1-913144-31-9

PENNILESS PRESS PUBLICATIONS
*Website :www. pennilesspress. co. uk/books*

# Contents

## SON BURNED

'Yes, I'm afraid it's positive.'

So there we are. The beginnings of a baby inside me. Now that it's a definite fact I feel relief. A relief to be free from hope. Funny sort of relief.

The grizzly drizzly Saturday evening continues. Little young ones look like little old ones. A grey wetness clings to coats, hair, trees.

In a cafe I smoke – how many? – maybe fourteen cigarettes. Three cups of coffee I swallow. Caffeine and nicotine should have soothed my shock by now.

To complete Operation Calm Down I poke about in the cluttered filing cabinet that is my mind.

The well-worn hand-out on Others In The Same Situation comes out for perusal.

So time passes in a cafe in Saturday evening O'Connell Street. A woman sits thinking of other women emerging from other doctors' rooms in Rialto, Clontarf and Addis Ababa at this precise moment. All fallen and unmarried. Maybe they'd have their heads chopped off in some countries. All burdened with results from bottles of wee-wee labelled 'Positive'.

Feeling I'm going to vomit. I lurch to the door. The street outside is wet.

I walk in the rain. After a while the sick feeling goes away. I see a shop swollen with girls searching for garments that will guarantee Real Love if combined with coloured eyelids and shining hair.

Automatically I move clothes along hangers. Without even trying it on I buy a yellow blouse.

Listen to this, beginnings of a baby: Tonight you and I will be clothed in gold. The city stinks of November but we will walk in a sunlight of the soul. We'll be as exotic and warm as the streets of Rimini.

Rimini is where you were conceived, my little one. I wonder will your eyes be brown. Will you call me Mama Mia? Some Mama, God help you.

It was the promise of the tan that did it. Cattolica. Follow the sun with Joe Walsh. Up every morning at dawn to try and beat the Germans to the deck chairs on the beach. If you jumped the queue on them they looked like they'd send you to Belsen. Stuck up against each other like sardines for that precious few feet of sand. Everyone sitting paralysed as the sun beat down on us, burning us like roast chickens.

And then the day he saw me from the pier.

'Melina Mercouri!' he shouted out. Everything else he said to me was Greek, or should I say Italian. I couldn't make head or tail of his rat- tat-tat sentences thrown at me a hundred miles an hour. Elaborate seduction techniques. And me stupid enough to think he liked me. Or thought I looked like Melina. Had to admit I was a bit like her in my bikini. Maybe it was the bikini he fell in love with.

The flat is filthy and cold. Breakfast dishes still piled on the table. To keep my spirits up I throw five firelighters into the grate. To deafen the silence I put on a tape. Light and sound can make even this drab place seem cheerful. *Brown Girl in the Rain* at full volume. I leap around, waving my arms in the air.

The music ends. I fling myself into the sunken-down sofa. Flames flicker into darkness. Fires need care and coal. I haven't the energy for either.

In the dark stillness the shock comes at me.

I'm pregnant.

Frantic search in the filing cabinet. This time it's a Questionnaire. Fast and furious I fling the questions at myself. The rapidity of my replies establishes my sanity.

Address? 323 Ranelagh Villas, Dublin 6.

Sex? Female, sometimes neuter.

Age? 27.

Occupation? Legal Secretary. Well it's better than being an illegal one, isn't it?

Job done, I start feeling anxious again. Heart pounding like a drum. Tongue too big for my mouth so I can't swallow. Hands hot and sweaty.

Let there be no panic. Every emergency covered. A few deep breaths to still the heart.

Check pulse. Already it's much slower. Too slow? No, normal you fool, normal.

Time for the mirror test. Pull down the skin under one of eyes. At the same time stick out tongue. Reflected in the mirror it looks just as a tongue should look. Maybe a little pale but pale is probably better than being too red. Too bloody could be high blood pressure. Who wants that in my condition? It causes clots.

What the hell am I going to do?

I could write to him. He should be told. It's not every day you start a baby in someone's belly. But where would I write to?

What was his name? Was it Luigi? Luigi what? Don't know.

'Dear Luigi with the green check shirt who took out the Irish girl on August15th. It was a very hot night. The girl had a lovely tan. She drank an awful lot of wine.'

Now that that's done, all I need to do is post it. How many hundreds of Luigis are there in Rimini? Hundreds of green check shirts. Hundreds of Irish girls with tans drinking wine. How many of them look like Melina?

What's the use. Poor baby, you only have me. God love you. A nice pallardy,

What will I tell them at home?

They'll notice at Christmas. No, they won't. Could be I've put on weight. I needn't go home till it's over. What will I do with it? Stop it, I can't tell them. It would kill them. Pull yourself together.

The blouse. Try on the blouse.

Looks very nice. Colour suits me. Never wore yellow before. Figure not too bad either. Thin if anything. But it won't take them long to notice at work. Girls can always tell.

I could leave. And do what?

Stop it. Keep moving. Action.

How about an old dance? Hey, beginnings of a baby, would you like to shake a leg? Suppose you haven't got a leg yet. Maybe a weeny toe. Poor little weeny toe in there.

Once in town I saw a child of about six. Must have been a thalidomide baby. They don't call it that anymore. He had a little baby's hand sticking from his shoulders. Poor baby. God I hope you're normal when you're born. Won't you be normal for me?

When I was a child I used to call it 'getting' a baby, like shoes or a doll. 'Hey, Maisie, is your Mammy getting a baby?'

Outside it's still raining. I feel a bit sick again. Will I throw up? No. Am I dying? Stop it, there's nothing wrong with you. Need more therapy.

Any ideas, pregnant lady?

Do the counties. They always relax you.

'Armagh, child.' The nun's face leers down at me.

'Yes, Sister. Armagh, Lurgan, Portadown.'

'Monaghan?'

'Monaghan. Clones and Carrickmacross.'

Can still taste the sick in my mouth. Have to stop. But you can't.

'Limerick?'

'Limerick, Rathkeale and Newcastlewest.'

Mammy and Daddy loved me when I rattled off all the counties. Wouldn't love me now though. The news would kill the two of them. Too old now for an illegal baby. No not illegal, Can't even remember words now. What the hell is it? Illegitimate.

4

How can a baby be illegitimate? I'm the illegitimate one. You had nothing to do with it, you poor thing.

'Roscommon, child.'

'Roscommon, Boyle and Elphin.'

Head swirls back to a night long ago. Paying for my ticket into the National Ballroom. Drowned to the skin. No memory of how I got into town. Probably walked all the way.

The dance floor is swarming with wriggling bodies. Everyone selling themselves. Promises they can't keep. The fair in Tuam was more honest. A right slave market here.

Hopes of meeting someone. Guy approaches me with beige trousers and bell bottoms. He has a car. A good job. Bliss for other sensible girls. I had to be different. Cowboys or sailors without a penny with blue faraway eyes for her ladyship.

Different now though. Haven't got confidence anymore, or a bevy of friends around me. The old me would have stood on the balcony surveying from a distance. Now I'm in the thick of it.

A Civil Servant from County Longford asks me to dance with him. He seems to like me. Tells me all about himself without me asking. Unusual these days.

He's called Jerry Horgan.

He's 24 years old.

He likes soccer.

He loves the band.

He's not crazy about his job.

And, miracle of miracles, he does have a car.

He's telling me some sort of a joke. Laughing so much he can hardly talk. I put on a smile for him, a plastic one.

If I wanted his company I probably wouldn't get it. Tonight I don't. Need to be on my own. When he asks me for another dance I tell him I'm with a friend. The old excuse.

In the toilet I throw up. A big deal for me. Haven't vomited since I got sick in a car at the age of fourteen.

Two girls at the mirror whisper about me. They think I'm drunk. Wish to God it was as simple as that. Well for ye, happy normal good girls. I'm a condition now.

Slip out into the night air. The rain is over. Poor new blouse all vomity and smelly now.

Sudden passion for a bag of chips. That's part of it, they say. Longings for particular foods.

Once I read in a story about a princess who had a desire for strawberries when she was pregnant. It was winter time. Her husband searched his kingdom for strawberries. Can't remember how it ended. Typical me.

Chips. Easily known I'm no princess. Must be the Italian influence. Briseann an dúchas trí shúile an chait, mar a déarfa.

Wonder is it the baby or me that has the craving? Hey you in there, here's a coincidence for you. I'm served with your first longing by your father's fellow countryman and he's wearing a green check shirt. Well golly, isn't it a small world. See the brave Mama you've got, Luigi. Into a chipper on her own and walking all the way to Ranelagh at a quarter past one in the morning.

Before I know it I'm home. Can I still call it home?

Don't feel like bed. After I lie down it will seem worse. That's when things always hit you.

I know what, I'll wash my hair. Good therapy to keep active. No I won't, it's too cold.

Some firelighters left in the box. I throw them into the grate with a wad of newspapers bundled up. Soon we have a merry blaze.

Would like to play music but better not put on a record. Your one downstairs will be giving out. Can imagine her reaction. Her and her steady boyfriend. And her engagement ring.

The three rings of marriage: engagement ring, wedding ring, suffer-ring. Ha ha. Would I like it? Do I even know?

What's the opposite to engaged?. Vacant, maybe. Like a toilet door.

How are you now, my little one?

Once I picked up a stone on the road from school and brought it home. Put it to bed in a matchbox with cotton wool for an eiderdown. Must have kept it for about three years. Wonder where it is now. Probably thrown out. Poor stone, you'd have been better off if I left you. Thought I was making you special by picking you up. Cut the crap. You're going back to your second childhood.

Wish I could ring someone. Who? Nobody at this time. Nobody to tell ever maybe.

More coffee. More cigarettes.

Probably bad for you in there, my little one. Make you smaller. Maybe even give you cancer.

Tomorrow I'll think about you. Tonight is mine.

That oul doctor one was a right pain in the neck. You'd think she'd be a bit better at it. Must have had to tell thousands like me. She knew some professional people it happened to. Imagine that. Teachers and solicitors having babies without husbands. What was the world coming to?

I floored her when she asked about the father. Some Italian, I said. Not too sure of the name.

She probably thought I was as hard as nails. Maybe I am. Haven't cried a tear yet. If I start I'll never stop.

This should be a happy occasion. What's up with me? Me that thought my pennies given to the teacher in Tuam were going to buy a black baby for me. Thought one day he'd arrive on the doorstep. Lovely little curls on him and shiny white teeth. Now I have one inside me that's mine and I'm up to ninety. One minus a husband, though. Aye, there's the rub.

God, it really will finish the pair of them.

'Cork, girl, the towns of Cork please.'

'Cork, Sister, Cork, Cobh, Bandon, Fermoy, Mallow, Youghal and Kinsale.'

'Okay, girl. Now what about Rimini?'

'Rimini, Sister? Afraid I'm not sure about that one. Is it a town or a county?'

'I don't know, girl.'

'Do they have counties in Italy, sister?'

'I don't know that either.'

Funny hearing the teacher say she doesn't know A first for me. And probably for her. Definitely needs to brush up on her Italian. (That sounds dirty).

Poor baby. Part of your heritage is lost. Ignorant Mama knows nothing of your fatherland. Or your father. What a mess.

What about my own parents? They're too old to take it. Wouldn't be too bad if there were a few married ones in the family. Sadly there's only me, the black sheep. Not even one little white one to ease the burden and shame.

One mistake and I end up like this. Is there any way out of it? Could have it scooped out, I suppose. Like a vacuum cleaner sucking up dust. They do it in an afternoon now. Used to be the mailboat but everything local now. Procedure on Saturday morning, back before work on Monday.

No, couldn't do that. I'll keep you, Luigi. Let's have another fag and another cup of coffee.

What will I tell them? That I wasn't thinking straight? That I wasn't thinking at all?

It wasn't what they'd planned for me. They wanted a husband, the ring, the house. All together like Brown's Cows. All part of one plan.

8

God, I'm jacked. Wish I could sleep. No point in getting into bed.

'Galway, girl?'

'Galway, Tuam and Ballinasloe, Sister.' Ballinasloe was where the mental hospital was. God help them, we used to say. The poor creatures, gone to Ballinasloe.

To hell with it. I'll wash the hair.

Water icy. Wouldn't you know. Now it'll take ages to dry. Blast it, no fags left. Maybe I'll get pneumonia from the wet head and die. No one would ever know then. I'd depart the world with my honour intact.

I wonder what you look like in there. Your poor little toe that went dancing and tasted chips.

Stop it.

God, I feel miserable.

'Louth, please.'

Ah good, we're back to the kind sister.

'Dundalk, Drogheda, Ardee and Carlingford.'

Wish I had another fag. Should probably start giving them up from now. Or from last week.

'Leitrim?'

'Leitrim, Manorhamilton and Mohill.'

Wonder would there be an all-night place where I could get a pack? Too cold to go out. No firelighters left either.

Lord, it's only bloody freezing. What a day. And I've told no one. Big Mouth has finally kept something to herself. Me that has five million friends to dish out advice to me. Long chats over whether I should cut my hair. Deep discussions on whether I'll go to Ballybunion or Bundoran for my holidays.

I'd cut my hair till I was bald and be a nun if this went away.

If I'm unpregnant, God, I'll give my life to others for ever and ever. Honest. Unpregnify me, please, I beg you. Some nun. One little scrap of a baby and you're whining like an oul one.

Big moon outside the window. Never thought such a day would turn into such a night. Looks like frost. Soon it will be Christmas. At least I'll get over that OK. I'll wear big jumpers and eat like a horse. That might cut off the insults

Wonder is it a sin if you don't remember. Drunkenness is a sin, I suppose.

Loss of control and self-respect. Let's go through the deadly sins. Pride, lust, anger, gluttony. Can't remember the other ones. Lust is the big one.

Sleeping with a man outside marriage. Deadly sin. Funny how we used to say a film was deadly. A hairdo could be deadly too, or a good film, but a deadly sin is talking about your soul and hellfire. Does anyone still talk about hellfire anymore?

What's done is done. No use rehashing the past. I'm tired. Might as well go to bed now.

'O Solo Mio,' I sing for my little lad.

A lullaby for you, darling.

And now to bed for me too.

Will be in the land of nod as soon as head hits pillow. Too tired to boil the kettle for a hot water bottle.

'Sligo?'

'Sligo, Collooney and Ballymote.'

Eyes closing. Hey, Luigi beag, your Mama Mia is a drunkard. Has no self-respect.

Once she lost the run of herself. Was lustful in Rimini. A man with brown eyes and a green check shirt.

He was gorgeous, though. And she got a lovely tan.

Will probably sleep now. I've actually survived the first day of knowing. Alone.

Well not quite alone. The two of us, Luigi.  Not alone with you inside me.  I have you, my little darling.

You, Luigi, and a lovely tan.

# LOVE

The spinster lady came. She shook the rain from her hair and body. Nobody saw her tender neck or her delicate hands.

She stood by the electric fire and steamed. The smell of rain reminded her of long ago when once she'd said to her mother, 'I'd love to go out and run in the rain with a bar of soap and to wash and have bubbles all over me.'

Her mother had replied, 'Such talk is sinful.' Everything was sinful to her mother, even talk itself. But she was long gone now so the spinster lady could stay out all night if she liked.

She made herself some tea and boiled an egg. Then from force of habit she washed up because mother said there was nothing worse than dirty cups left gathering dust.

She looked out at the night. The avenue was quiet. Bare trees stood nakedly leaning out to her. She loved them as she always had. She hated cluttered-up dressings on trees. And on people. She wanted to take off all her clothes and run out in the rain and wind. 'I'm the original streaker,' she told herself. And she smiled.

The spinster lady was in a strange mood that night. The smell of the rain and the stark trees brought back sensations to her that she'd forgotten ever existed. She was eighteen years old again and she wanted to stay up all night, not put in rollers and not put out the light or get a good night's sleep. She wanted excitement.

But spinster ladies of 51 years don't get much excitement. For one thing there are barriers preventing them from entering places of entertainment. The young can congregate in warm lounge bars. Comfortable couples of 82 years can be smiled on in such places. Bachelors gay (or even not gay) of 108 can be one of the boys. But spinster ladies of 51 years are unacceptable.

To hell with it, she said to herself, I'm going out.

She pinned up her hair with pins and looked at herself in the mirror. No, she thought. Then she pulled them out again. She let the grey and brown stripes envelop her neck and shoulders.

She went out into the night hell-bent , or heaven bent, on having a good time. As the bus took her into town she thought of how much a creature of habit she'd become. It was now ten

past ten and unthinkable that Miss Cleary should be riding on a bus to the city hell-bent on pleasure.

On pleasure, on brandy, on a happy evening. These were the words her heart sang.

'You have the change of life over you,' said her reason, 'You're the typical old maid now, you're finished.' But then another song came into her as the bus danced along.

'I've never had a life so I've never changed.' sang her heart, 'And tonight I'm going to start one.'

She walked bravely up the stairs of the Golden Goblet. She made her way to the counter.

'A double brandy please,' said Miss Cleary in a very loud voice. Soon she was wrapped in a haze of warmth.

She didn't notice the nudges of the couples beside her, or the sniggers of the bright young things down the bar, or even the crude remarks of the bachelors gay.

The warmth of the bar was all she was aware of. The shining glasses. The soft lights.

This is heaven, she thought as she let the syrupy liquid slide down her throat. Then she had another one. Now, she thought, now I feel complete.

But when she got up off her stool to leave the bar she fell. Down the stairs tumbled Miss Cleary and her glasses case shattered.

Three people – one a retired civil servant, one a Miss Marilyn McDonald from Accounts in Murphy & Gunn, and one a fellow of the student variety – were shocked to see her warm pink drawers (they were obviously seconds) and her knobbly knees.

She'd rolled into a puddle at the bottom of the stairs.

A crowd gathered around her to discuss her.

She was vaguely aware of many voices. Then the voices stopped and she heard a car engine. She found herself being cradled into a seat.

She didn't know that it was the young man of the student variety who'd put her into a taxi and given the driver his last euro. She didn't know he'd found her address by looking at her glasses case. She didn't know a thing about the journey home.

The next thing she knew was that she was indeed home, because when she looked around her she saw all the things that were familiar to her – the door that squeaked when you opened it, the slightly worse-for-wear carpet, a cup on the sink with some cold tea still in it.

She was very drunk.

She made her way to the bathroom.

She pulled some neat towels from the rail and flung the red facecloth, mother's, up to the ceiling. Eventually she came into contact with a big bar of soap. She tried to wash herself but the soap kept falling from her onto the floor. She was too groggy to chase it.

It's time to go out again, she thought.

So she was off on her travels again.

Pulling off her clothes, she ran like a mad person out into the rain.

It poured down on her. Soap bubbles ran into gutters. She tightly wrapped her arms around a poor thin brown tree and sang to it.

This is the song she sang.

*'Are you lonely, my little baby? Mammy has come to mind you. I'm sorry I left you for a while. Your father was a vulgar man. He went away and left me all alone and I had to give you up.*

*I know the orphanage was bleak and awful and I know you missed your mammy but I'm here now. I'll give you shelter and protection from all of them. From all of them with their families and their engagement rings and their cheap jokes. Mammy will comb your dear brown hair.*

*And did you eat your porridge today, love? If you didn't it doesn't matter. Your mammy will smile and let her little girl have cornflakes even if it's winter time.'*

That was the song. Then she sang another one:

*'I have a treat for you, my love. Mammy and you will go the pictures after school this evening. We'll leave the dirty dishes and you and your Mammy will buy you two boxes of Smarties and three Milky Ways and we'll sit at the pictures like two friends and we'll laugh in the dark at the lovers on the screen and the lovers in the audience. Your Mammy doesn't think such things are dirty and doesn't think you should be protected from seeing them because she loves her little girl . We'll wait for the film two times over if you wish and I have millions of other treats for you as well.'*

The rain was still pouring down as she finished her song. Her body was exposed to the wind and cold but because she'd drunk so much she felt nothing.

She sang to the tree about how her baby could bring in her friends in the evening and how when she was old enough she could mix with the boys and have parties. She sang of all the

things her mother had told her were bad. And she told her baby she was pretty and that she was going to have great times. She never mentioned sin or never told her baby about the one thing all men are out for.

Miss Cleary was thin. Miss Cleary was greying. Miss Cleary was typical of spinster ladies. But tonight she was a fat warm Mama in a flowery apron baking cakes for her daughter's 21st birthday party. Tonight she was someone to run to. Tonight she was more motherly than all of the mothers in all the houses on all the avenue.

Paddy Grogan, a night worker, saw her at 7.10 a.m. She was sitting at the bottom of a tree without any clothes on. He wrapped his coat around her and telephoned Dr. Ward. That was his local GP, a small man with a bald head and a funny mouth.

In no time at all, Dr. Ward arrived to examine her. As soon as he looked at her he feared things were bad.

'This woman has no pulse,' he said to Paddy Grogan. Paddy looked at him as if to say, 'What am I supposed to do about that?'

Was it possible she'd passed away on this drunken rainy night?

'Hold on,' said Dr. Ward, 'I think I feel something.'

Miss Cleary had survived. Dr Ward phoned for an ambulance. She was taken to a psychiatric hospital to be treated.

The day ran on. The world returned to normal. People went to work and did ordinary things. That night, Paddy Grogan told his friends in the pub all about her in the pub. Some of the other people who'd seen her at the bottom of the stairs talked about her too.

What had happened to this batty old woman? She'd had two stiff drinks. Now she was in an asylum. Could it be that simple?

There were many who gave their opinions on what caused such a tragic eventuality. Sexual frustration was the most popular cause attributed.

When children were out of the room, sensible men told their equally sensible wives about a stark naked Miss Cleary hanging onto a tree.

'I think she was a bit nuts,' said Mr Geraghty, an intelligent man by all reports, 'but then she was a spinster.'

'What a shame,' said his wife. 'I wish she had my problems. You know what I mean, someone to worry about except herself. She was probably too selfish. A typical old maid. Thank God none of the kids saw her.'

'And her mother was such a lady,' Mrs O'Dea added.

Huddles of women sniggered in the supermarket the next morning.

John Kelly, the manager, said: 'It's not the same way we all go, thanks be to God.'

In twenty places of employment twenty men told an average of ten co-workers about her. Soon the whole north side of the city had the story.

Miss Cleary developed double pneumonia and for a while it looked as if she mightn't survive but in the end she did.

She has now realised, after many pills and some other procedures that were performed on her in a room with green walls in the outer suburbs, that she's in the right place for her condition.

She's still being treated for her nerves and the doctors are unanimous that it is indeed an obvious case of sexual frustration.

'The fact of the soap points to religious scruples,' said a trained psychologist, 'and the contact with the tree is inhibited sex.'

'When she leaves the hospital,' Paddy Grogan said, 'she'll be on heavy doses of Valium and Librium and all other kinds of iums that are manufactured to help misfits stay within the law so innocent children can be protected from them.'

The young man of the student variety sometimes wonders whatever happened to the gentle-faced woman with the shy smile and the warm pink drawers, seconds at a reduced rate.

# A CHANCE MEETING

She knew she was no spring chicken. More of a summer hen she supposed. Forty five wasn't *that* old, was it? Yes it was.

The hair was dyed, the waist more or less gone. A bunion protruded from her left foot. Little worry lines were starting to sprout around her eyes.

'The good news,' she joked, 'is that my teeth are my own. I paid for them.' Ha ha. The old ones were the best.

By and large (emphasis on the large) she told herself, she wasn't too bad.

Such were her thoughts as she looked out of the bus window at Fairview. The evening was still and beginning to get dark. In front of her were two young girls. Painted and tarted-up for the night. Well for them. They'll learn. Not all beer and skittles.. They have it all before them, she thought.

Opposite her was a worried-looking oul one with dyed red hair and her fingers all brown from smoking. Little birdy legs that hardly reached the floor. Musha, God love her, the trials and tribulations of life were written all over her pinched little mouth. Probably gives the husband a dog's life. Probably drives him to drink as well. 'What hour is this to be coming in three sheets in the wind?' she'd say. The poor devil. Wasn't he entitled to his few drinks to escape Birdy Legs? Imagine waking up to that kisser every morning.

She became conscious of the person beside her. Out of the corner of her eye she could see him reading a letter. It began, 'Dear Reginald.'

Reginald. The name suited him. He looked like a retired brigadier general type.

He was very well dressed. Beige twills. Well at least she thought you called them twills. Beige twills sounded nice. He had a sort of rough tweedy jacket she just loved.

He reminded her of a Bruce or Bradley out of a Mills & Boon book. A type that would look good smoking a pipe. Greying at the temples and a walrus moustache on his gob. How was this the song went from Granny's windy-up gramophone? 'When he twirls his dark mustachio.' *South American Joe* name of the song

Now she was in another world.

*He took her in his arms. They were muscly. The smell of musk and the great outdoors aroused her. Feelings she never knew she had enveloped her. She could feel his manhood throbbing. 'Oh God. Reginald. Oh Reginald, Reginald.' 'Hush, hush my lovely. Not so hasty, my little dove. Hush hush, the night is long. We shall make love. Gently. The secrets of my heart will be yours. Gently sweet passionate bird.' 'Lie still my heart. Reggie, oh Reggie, can this be heaven?'*

'Next stop the terminus.'

Feck. Back to reality with a bang.

But then, unbelievably, Reginald spoke.

'Excuse me, young woman,' he said in this big American twang. Young, mind you. Thanks for that anyway.

'Yes?'

'Could you direct me to O'Connell?'

He obviously hailed from somewhere south of the border. He certainly wasn't from Castleisland. Probably Alabama. Sounded posh too. Might have had black servants. The cotton fields back home. Carry me back to old Virginia.

'O'Connell Street? Of course. Actually I'm going that way myself.'

'Even better!' said Reginald.

They walked up Talbot Street side by side. It was quiet at this time of the day. As they crossed the road at the corner of Gardiner, as he would put it, he took her arm.

'Careful, my dear.'

*Oh the masterful air of him. The gentle touch. The caring. The sharing. The whole being that was Reginald. In that moment she knew. She knew Reginald would be hers for all time.*

'Here we are. O'Connell Street.'

They were outside the Gresham. The place looked tailor-made for Reginald. He cleared his throat.

'I hope I'm not out of line here,' he said, 'but would you care to join me for a drink?'

Yes, yes, yes, a little voice inside her said. .

'Well I don't know. I'm actually meeting a friend, but not for another hour. Yes. Maybe. Why not? I suppose it would be okay.'

'Wonderful.'

Was she doing the right thing? Of course she was. This could be the beginning of her new life. Down on the plantation with Reginald. Carry me back to old Virginia.

.    They walked into the foyer of the hotel. As they did so she sensed a lot of eyes, especially female ones, eating up Reginald. In those moments he owned the place.

They sat down at a table.

'And now my dear, what's your poison, if I may.'

'A glass of white wine would be lovely.'

She could almost taste it already. She was getting drunk on the expectation.

He went up to the counter to order it. When he came back he looked at her as if she was the only woman in the world.

They sat opposite each other.

*Strangers, yet for both the recognition of a life-long search ended. There was no need for words. They both knew. Knew in some faraway primitive part of their beings. This was it. Love had come to town.*

'This is my first visit to Dublin,' said Reginald. 'Indeed, my first visit to Ireland. Isn't that something? And I must say I'm having a blast of a time. People so friendly and the climate just to my taste. Sadly, not a leprechaun in sight.'

She must have put on a face because he stopped there.

'I'm kidding, of course. We know that stuff is blarney.'

'Maybe not,' she hazarded. Reginald burst out laughing.

He looked around him at the chandelier, the fancy furnishings.

'Ireland sure is booming big time,' he said. Did Reginald not read the papers? Did he not know we were now in a recession? She felt like saying, 'Not in Sean McDermott Street around the corner it ain't,' but she didn't. She couldn't burst Reginald's bubble.

He cleared his throat again.

'Sorry, my dear,' he said, 'We haven't introduced ourselves. My name is Reginald, Reginald J. Oppenheimer, Attorney-at-Law, Kentucky.'

*Well now, a lawyer. She hadn't been too far off. Why didn't they call them solicitors? She read somewhere that soliciting in America meant some kind of misbehaving. Funny, that.*

*He was from the Deep South. It seemed to her that they'd been together in some other time. Some far off place where lovers meet.*

*At last, the real thing.*

'And you are?'

'Eloise,' she said, though her name was actually Betty Barry.

'Gee, what a lovely name. Sounds French.'

'Yes, I'm part French on my mother's side'.

You couldn't say Betty Barry to a man like this on such a night. Her devotion to him deserved more than Betty feckin' Barry.

He told her of his work in Alabama, the Corporate Lawyer firm he worked for. How he was visiting the Celtic Tiger on business.

'And you my dear, what do you do?

'I'm an accountant,' she said, 'with a big firm here in the city.'

There was no need to tell him she was a typist for the past 25 years, working for one man in a dingy office in Palmerstown. How could Reginald Oppenheimer fall in love with Betty Barry the lowly typist?

He ordered some more wine. They chatted. The time flew. She forgot an appointment she'd made with her friend Marian O'Mahony. When Reginald excused himself to go to the men's room she got herself a large whiskey. She poured it into the wine glass just in case he came out suddenly. She had it gone in two seconds.

As she waited for Reginald to re-emerge, she pictured him talking to the night porter before he whisked her upstairs to the bridal suite.

He would be discreet. He would tip generously. A man of the world.

*Alone in the hotel room while the neon lights flashed in on them they made love until the early hours. Tomorrow they would visit Wicklow and she would show him the garden of Ireland. Soon they would be back in Alabama. She would laze about in the pool while Reggie - , Reginald to the world, but Reggie to her - busied himself doing his important work in the city. They would entertain at weekends and she would visit the beauty parlour every other Thursday. She would be a lady who lunched and everybody, just everybody, would marvel at her success. In the summers she might even run charity concerts for the rich and famous.*

'Fancy another, Eloise?'

'Well yes, perhaps. Just the one.'

They sipped their drinks and he told her more about his life, all the fascinating clients he represented. The whole hotel was looking at her, at them, envying her luck.

She felt as though she and Reginald had been together for thirty years or more. Oh, the romance of it. The thrill.

*Had the twins right off, they did. Junior was top of the baseball league at Vasser and little Missie was married to an oil baron in Dallas. Getting to be quite the boring old parents, weren't they? Snaps always ready to show to people in both of their wallets. Missie pregnant now as well. Expecting her first next October. Where had the time gone? It seemed just like yesterday when she and Reggie met on that bus somewhere in Dublin in 2009.*

'Good golly, Eloise, you're such good company. Time has just flown by. Thanks for a lovely evening. The Irish are such a friendly people.'

She was wondering how he was going to go about making another date when she had the vague sense of his attention wandering.

A woman entered the hotel. A woman who looked at Reginald as if she knew him. What was going on here?

Reginald looked over at her.

'Ah here she comes at last. Meet my lovely wife, Eloise.'

He stood up. Betty's heart started to race, then falter.

'Clara darling,' he said, 'meet Eloise. She's been such a dear. So friendly, like all the Irish,. Did you enjoy the show, honey? Clara has been at the theatre, Eloise.'

Betty felt as if she'd been hit by a rock. She looked the infiltrator up and down.

Clara was tall and well preserved. Fifty if she was a day, thought Betty. Dreary bookish type with her grey hair tied back in a bun.

'Pleased to meet you, Eloise. Thank you so much for looking after Reginald. He isn't into theatre but I had to see the Abbey. Would never have forgiven myself getting on the plane back home if I didn't. Bit of a culture vulture I am. Quite a good play, my dear. You'd have enjoyed it so must, that's presuming you understood it. A comedy of manners, I daresay.'

So this was the deal. If she understood it. What a nerve. As if she was Einstein herself. Herself and her stupid hubbie. Didn't even know about the recession. Absolutely no taste in clothes. Talk about dowdy. No make-up either, a right old stick-in-the-mud.

Betty glared at her. There was silence. Reginald cleared his throat. Eventually Clara put on her gloves.

'Well, birdie must fly,' she said, 'Places to go and people to meet and all that, you know. Reg, be a doll and check out the cab numbers, will you?'

Reginald dug into his pocket. He produced a shrivelled up taxi guide. He handed her a number and she dialled it on her mobile.

'Well anyway,' she said to Betty, 'nice to meet you. Maybe our paths will cross again sometime. Happy trails.'

Betty felt light in the head. She didn't know if she was going to faint or not. Reginald gave her a half wave and then he was gone. With his lady love. His bloody stuck up wife.

She was on the street now. She stood inside the awning of the Savoy Cinema trying to recover her strength. She imagined Clara telling Reginald her views on the play all the way back to their hotel room in the 'cab.'

After a minute she buttoned her coat and checked herself in a mirror. She thought she felt ready to face the world again, a Reginald-free world.

She walked back down O'Connell Street hardly seeing the people or the traffic. There was a queue of people at the bus stop and they started shoving against her. She knew that was a sign one was due. Like cattle at a mart they were. What was the rush? She'd have laid bets it would only be half full at this time of night anyway. People were such brutes.

Then she saw one. It swished into the stop and she was carried along with the queue in a tide.

By the skin of her teeth she just fitted on.

The same overweight  driver that was on the earlier bus took her money.

She went towards the back seat and fell into it. As the bus passed through Fairview she became aware of two lovers wrapped around each other.

A skinny little woman snuggled up to a fat man with thighs bursting out of his shabby blue trousers. Love's young dream.

She hardly remembered getting off the bus or walking home. She just remembered being there, her head still sizzling with wine. She thought of Reginald, the play, the fussy wife. They were welcome to each other.

That night she didn't read her Mills & Boon to bring on sleep. She cried into her pillow instead.

The following morning a hungover Betty Barry felt like she'd been hit by a truck. She rang in sick.

'I'll be in in a few days,' she told her boss, 'I must have caught a bit of a bug.'

'They say it's going round,' he said, 'Mind yourself.'

'Don't worry,' she thought as she put down the receiver. 'I'll take care of No. 1.' Then she made a hot mug of tea for herself.

After she finished it she went back to bed. As she nodded off she thought she heard the vague drone of a Boeing 707 roaring its way back across the Atlantic. Probably carrying Reginald and Clara inside it, she thought. They were welcome to each other.

She didn't feel too bad. She'd been invited to a wedding the following week. That was the thing about life. You never knew what it was going to throw up.

# KEEP TAKING THE TABLETS

When Francis Farrelly gave up his medication he became a man of moods. If you got him on a good day there was nobody more pleasant, more chatty. You might be a total stranger but if he happened to sit beside you on a bus or train he'd engage you in conversation, regaling you with stories of his childhood in Roscommon, maybe, or if you were a member of the fair sex complimenting you on your appearance.

He made a point of sussing out women's good points. Some had a particular colour in their eyes that he would describe as a cornflower blue, maybe, or dusky brown, or maybe they had a profile that he would say he'd like to have sketched for posterity if he were an artist.

Maybe it was a trim figure he would admire saying the young lady in question was more shapely than a model on the catwalk.. Or he might even compliment a woman on her rosebud mouth or her beautiful white teeth.

Most ladies reacted well to these compliments because Francis was a refined and well-dressed man and never did they feel he was making a move on them. He was 65 years old and he always took great care to inform the lady in question that he and Mrs Farrelly were married over forty years. All their little birds had flown the nest, he would add, so they were now just a good old-fashioned Darby and Joan.

If you met Francis on a bad day, however, he could be a holy terror. Take for example the way he would be if he was in one of his moods and you met him on the 31A bus into town.

'Move over there,' he might say to the lady beside him, or, if she was a bit on the large side, 'You're taking up the whole seat, Missus, is it twins you're expecting now?' (And this to someone who would be well past childbearing age).

Or he might say to a lady with an elongated nose, 'Where in God's earth did you get a hooter like that? God love you, you'd frighten the crows.'

On such days ladies would sit mortified beside him if they were shy or elderly. Younger girls would tell him where to get off. They'd let fly a string of obscenities at him. On three different occasions the driver had to stop the bus and call the Gardai.

When he was brought to the Garda station the Gardai would phone his house. Mrs Farrelly would have to drag her arthritic knees off the fireside chair, interrupting her soaps, to answer the phone. Later on she'd go down to the station to collect him. She'd try to explain to the guards that her husband suffered from his nerves. After a while they'd scratch their heads in bewilderment. They usually let him off with yet another warning, realising the poor fella was a little bit strange.

Mrs Farrelly was a small butt of a woman. 'Here's me head, the rest of me is following,' she'd say. The expression fitted her perfectly. She was always a bit on the plump side. After she got the problems with her knees the weight poured onto her even more.

She had a round little moon of a face with a high colour and two buttony brown eyes like raisins sunk into her pink cheeks. Her hair had gone grey when she was just forty but she used a red henna dye on it. To be honest, the red of her hair clashed with her brightly-coloured cheeks and the whole picture was a little bit harsh on the eye.

Mr Farrelly couldn't have been more different. He was thin in frame and still sported a fine head of coal-black hair. Some people said he used a dye like his wife but he denied this. He also had all his own teeth. Mrs Farrelly had most of hers removed when she was in Primary School. The ones that remained gave her no end of problems. As she fattened out, her gums got larger. She was always having to change her dentures. Sometimes she didn't bother with them, leaving them in a mug on the bathroom shelf.

Mr Farrelly didn't mind about such things. In his eyes she was still the same Lottie Cunningham he'd met at a dance in Ballintubber when she was just sixteen. She was a lively little thing then without a pick of flesh on her and two merry eyes dancing in her head. He remembered her jiving around the floor like a whirlwind. Her plump thighs showing. Her whole body gyrating to the beat of the hucklebuck. He fell in love with her the first time he'd seen her. The feeling was mutual.

They married in the early 1970s and moved to Dublin to a flat in Drumcondra. Mr Farrelly got called to the Civil Service and was placed in the Department of Social Welfare in an office over Busaras. After a while they got a mortgage and took up residence in a three-bedroomed house. It was a semi-detached in Raheny, close to the Dart with schools and churches nearby.

Lottie gave birth to two children in the next three years, a boy and a girl. They named the boy John Joe after a grand-uncle. He'd died young in America from pneumonia. The poor fellow was found dead in a dirty apartment building in Boston. The girl was called Amanda Jane. Lottie once read a childhood book about a sweet child of that name. She called her after her.

The children were well-behaved. They did as their parents told them and grew into fine young adults. John Joe was now an area manager for a supermarket in Cork. Amanda Jane had married a French man she met when she was working as an *au pair*. She was living in an apartment block outside Paris.

Francis' moods weren't so noticeable when he was a young man, though he did at one time have a breakdown. This occurred when he was in his early thirties. He was hospitalised for three months in St. Patrick's psychiatric hospital as a result. He was put on medication and that stabilised him. His moods improved considerably in the next few months and Lottie was much relieved. He wasn't exactly dancing with joy, she told people, but he was predictable. 'Like a quiet November day,' she liked to say.

He continued taking his medication for many years until he retired from the Civil Service. He got a nice severance package for leaving early. His problem was largely to do with stress in the workplace. He saw no point in taking tablets now that he was free of that. Indeed, his reason for early retirement was exactly that pressure. Younger men and women were adept with computers and modern technology but he wasn't. His confidence evaporated and he dreaded going to work.

They gave him a great send-off in the office. Lottie bought herself a new outfit in Clery's to fit the occasion. It was as good as anything the mother of a bride might have. It was made of a blue brocade material with the skirt just skimming her knees. She managed to squeeze her right foot (the bunioned one) into a dainty pair of high-heeled shoes for the night. These were wider fitting but looked very fashionable.

After an hour she was able to remove the right shoe and hide her feet under the table until it was time to leave. Lottie didn't let a drop of alcohol pass her lips that night, then of course she had taken the pledge at her Confirmation and had kept that pledge all her life, but Francis got 'nicely'. He rolled into bed a free happy man at 3.15 a.m.

But that was many years ago. Retirement took its toll on him just as work had. As Lottie once put it, 'sometimes not working is harder on the nerves than working.' 'Too true,' Francis agreed. The days became too long for him to pass and he didn't have enough friends or hobbies to help him along. 'I'm wishing my life away,' he told Lottie. Lottie wrung her hands in despair. She just didn't know what to do with him.

It so happened that one night in late October 2007, Francis found himself in a particularly bad state. He was like a caged rat, going around the house from room to room without apparent purpose. Poor Lottie was installed in front of the television watching *Emmerdale*, her favourite programme. She knew the characters in it as well as those in her own family. She was enjoying it immensely and looking forward to the half-time break when she'd go upstairs for a bar of peppermint cream chocolate. She always kept this t on hand as she found it soft and easy on her gums.

'For God's sake, Francis, will you sit still,' she said when her husband came stamping into the room for the fifth time in ten minutes, 'I can't concentrate on my programme.'

'Get up the yard with your programme,' he said, 'Have some sense, woman, and stop watching that trash. These people are actors. It's not real life.'

'For me it is,' Lottie responded, 'If you don't like it you can lump it. Go off somewhere for yourself and don't be bothering me.'

'I'll go into town so,' Francis huffed, 'I can't take much more of this. I feel a weight of worry on my chest. My heart is palpitating. I have a vile taste in my mouth.'

'Is that all?' Lottie said.

'Now that you mention it,' Francis continued, 'No it isn't. I also see no point in living. My fingers are tingling, I have dizzy sensations and I'm constipated.'

Normally Lottie would have been sympathetic to him but she was so engrossed in the soap she couldn't give him the sympathy he needed.

'I'm sick listening to your complaints,' she said, 'Cop on to yourself. You're as fit as a fiddle. It's your nerves. Go back on the tablets and you'll be grand.'

Francis marched out of the room at that. His wife settled back into her *Emmerdale*.

Time passed. The programme finished. Then *Coronation Street* came on. She liked that too but not as much. When everything was over she felt bad about what she'd said to her husband. She knew it wasn't his fault that he'd raised his voice to her. He needed to see the doctor and go back on his pills. Maybe it was just a phase he was going through - though admittedly a long one. She shouldn't have taken it personally.

Lottie thought she heard the door bang during the middle of *Coronation Street*. She assumed it was Francis coming back from his walk. She doubted he had gone into town. He often said that as a kind of threat but he usually only went round the block to clear his head.

She decided she'd put on a nice lamb chop to make up for being hard on him. When it was done she called his name but there was no answer. She thought he might have gone to bed for a lie-down. He often did that when he was feeling low.

When she went up to the bedroom he wasn't there. It was now getting dark. It was wet and windy outside as well. Lottie started to worry.

There was no sign of him by eleven and by now she'd worked herself up into a frenzy. She phoned John Joe in Cork at twenty past eleven in a hysterical state.

'I'm worried about your father,' she said.

'Don't be ridiculous, Mam,' he told her. 'It's more than likely he went for a drink. He'll probably be home on the last bus. Sit down and relax yourself. Dad is fine. Make yourself a cup of tea. He'll be home before the kettle is boiled.'

Lottie made herself five cups of tea. She worked herself into a state walking round the house and peering out the window. It seemed hours before she finally heard the key in the lock.

'Oh my God,' she said, 'I was about to call the guards. Where were you? I was on to John Joe. The poor lad is in a state.'

'The guards? So you thought I'd been misbehaving again.'

'I was worried you might have had an accident or fallen somewhere.'

'From drink?'

'I mean a bad footpath or something. Or maybe you'd been attacked. You know what things are like nowadays. Why are you arguing with me? It's been a nightmare worrying about you.'

'You know me. I'm always arguing with everybody.'

'No you're not.'

'I am. For God's sake lay off me. If I say I'm arguing, I'm arguing.'

Lottie didn't know how to deal with him when he was like this. If she suggested something he might go for her and if she said nothing he might accuse her of not caring. It was an awkward one.

'Maybe you should go back on the pills,' she chanced saying after a minute.

'Do you think I need to?' He was still being aggressive.

'I'm only trying to help. I think you need them.'

'All right, I'll go back on them. Are you happy now? Maybe I'll take an overdose and put us all out of our misery.'

Lottie started to cry. Big fat tears rolled down her cheeks

'I'm sorry,' he said, 'I didn't mean to upset you.'

. She was hoping he'd come over and put his arms around her but he just said quietly, 'I have a confession to make.'

She didn't know what was coming. She could feel her heart beating fast.

'What kind of a confession?'

He went over to the cupboard and took out a bottle of whiskey. He raised it to his lips and took a swig out of it.

'I was with a woman tonight.'

Her mouth went dry and her heart started to pound.

'A woman?'

'Yes, a woman. You know what women are. The opposite of men.'

'Are you telling me you're having an affair?'

'I didn't say that.'

'What do you mean so?'

Francis took another swig of the whiskey and looked hard at his wife.

'Something is happening to us, Lottie,' he said, 'Something has been happening to us for a long time.'

'I don't know what you're talking about.'

'I know you don't,' he said, 'That's half the problem. Because you're so obsessed with the house and John Joe and Amanda Jane and your clothes and your friends and most of all your bloody awful soaps.'

Lottie started crying again.

'I don't know what you're on about. You've never said any of this to me before. '

'That doesn't mean I haven't thought it.'

'So that's why you were out with a woman.'

'You can take it whatever way you like.'

He was almost quarter way down the whiskey bottle now. She was beginning to wish he'd stayed out, or that she'd been in bed asleep when he came in.

'I'll stop talking about clothes and the house and the family,' she blurted out, 'and I'll throw the bloody television out the window if you want. I don't care about the soaps. What I care about is you. And you being with a woman.'

He put the drink down.

'The woman meant nothing,' he said.

'Did you sleep with her?'

'No, I just talked to her.'

She began to calm down.

'I don't know why you would call that a confession.'

He put on a disturbed expression, the kind of expression she hadn't seen since all those years ago when he was in St. Patrick's.

'I called it a confession because I felt more real talking to her than I've felt with you for a long time.'

'Oh Francis, that's one of the most hurtful things you've ever said to me.' She was sobbing loudly now.

'Too bad. There it is.'

'Are you saying it's my fault?' she sobbed.

'Maybe it's both of our faults. Or none of our faults. Maybe we've let the ground grow under our feet.'

'Maybe we have, Francis, but now that you've told me that, and that I've been blind to it, maybe we can do something about it.'

He put the whiskey away and came over to her.

'When was the last time we were out together, Lottie,' he asked her, 'When was the last time we did anything together?'

'I don't know, Francis. I don't think about things like that. Women are different than men. You said you loved me. I thought that was enough.'

'Maybe it is, Lottie. I do love you. But maybe sometimes we do the same things so often, life becomes a drudge. We forget we love each other.'

'I never forget I love you, Francis, not even for a second.'

Francis did put his arms around her. He held her tightly until her crying stopped. A long time seemed to elapse. She was aware of the silence of the night, a silence broken only by the ticking of the grandfather clock in the corner of the room.

He kissed her.

'Dry your eyes. You know it upsets me when you cry.'

'You've hurt me a lot tonight, Francis, but I know you'd never do that on purpose. I understand you. I've always understood you. But will you do me one favour? Will you tell me if you ever stop loving me, or if there's anything you see me doing that you don't like, or that you think might be bad for us?'

Francis smiled at her.

'Lottie,' he said, 'I don't mean to hurt you, I'm just a bit low. If I ever forget to tell you I love you, just give me a good slap'.

'I will,' she laughed.

'It's myself I'm angry with tonight, not you. That's why I flew off the handle. And that's why I spent the night talking to another woman.'

'Don't be talking to other women,' she said, 'talk to your wife and don't mind anyone else.'

'I promise I will', he said.

'I suppose she was young,' Lottie continued, 'young and skinny and better looking than  me.'

'She wasn't.'

'If I met her I'd sort her out. A right bit of goods trying to chat up another woman's husband.  No shame.  I know the  type.  The exact same thing happened in *Emmerdale* last week.'

Now it was Francis' turn to laugh.

'She was a woman in her sixties, Lottie.  We just got chatting in the pub. It was the fact that she listened to me that drew me to her, nothing else. She was lonely. We just passed the time together.'

Lottie went quiet for a few moments.

'In her sixties.  Alone in the pub.  Francis, she was probably a prostitute.  God help you, she could have dragged you back to some dingy room and taken all your money.  That happened in *Fair City* last month. Thank God you got away from her. You're not fit to be out on your own. The worry you put me through.  I was about to phone Amanda Jane in Paris.  Can you imagine how that would have upset her, not to mention Samuel and the two little ones.'

'Jesus Christ,' he said, 'I can't believe you'd want to go phoning people half way round the world because I went out for a few hours. Maybe it's you that needs the tablets.'

'Go on out of that, you trickster you,' she said, 'Go on up to bed and I'll bring you up a nice lamb chop I've cooked for you. I'll put it under the grill and have it reheated in a few minutes.'

As Francis looked at his wife, all the worry lines disappeared from her face. She wiped away her tears and went over to the cooker. As she fussed around the kitchen he saw her as Lottie Cunningham again in that dance-hall in Ballintubber all those years ago.

'I was thinking maybe it'd be a good idea if we took a holiday', he said. 'Maybe we could go to England. We could bring the car and visit the Lake District. A second honeymoon. We both loved it there.'

'That's a great idea, Francis. We need a holiday and the Lake District is just the ticket.'

Francis went up the stairs humming a tune to himself. . He was tucked up in bed when Lottie brought him up his chops fifteen minutes later. She fussed over him as she put the tray down on the bed, fluffing up his pillows.

She sat watching him devouring his food.

'Was she a young sixty,' she asked, 'I mean the woman in the pub?'

'Are we back to that again?'

'Those types that drink alone usually get very wrinkled from hard drinking. It's because I never touched a drop in my life, that I look so good.'

'She was wrinkled like a prune,' said Francis, 'She had no shape at all to her, she had bony knees and she was all painted up like a clown. Now are you happy?'

The reality was that the woman was beautiful, probably in her early fifties, They'd shared a few drinks but he couldn't tell Lottie that. She'd have fallen apart.

He knew if he asked her out she'd have accepted. Her name was Vera. He thought it suited her. Maybe he should have taken her

36

number. A few drinks now and then wouldn't have been meant anything. It was good to be with a woman who took a drink. She could talk too. He'd forgotten his love for Thomas Hardy until Vera mentioned *The Mayor of Casterbridge* and *Jude the Obscure*. He knew he should get back to his reading.

Vera a prostitute! Francis smiled at the thought. Nothing could have been farther from the truth. She was a lady, a lady down to her fingernails, her neatly-clipped fingernails. Her grey hair was lovely too. The streaks made her look genteel. Much better in its natural state than the gaudy styles most other women of her age had.

It was a pity Lottie didn't read or take a drink, Francis thought as he finished his chop.

'What are you thinking about?' Lottie asked him, 'You've gone very quiet.'

'I was thinking what a lovely chop it was,' Francis replied.

Lottie used to sit sipping her bitter lemon the few nights she did join him for a drink. Her expression was always one of suffering. Every few minutes she'd check her watch. This made Francis almost choke over his drink. She always wanted to leave the pub early.

A man needed to savour his drink, thought Francis, to look around him. Take in the atmosphere. Talk about intelligent things to a woman who appreciated such things.

Vera, yes indeed the name did the name suitd her. It sounded like veracity. Veracity meant truth. It probably came from the Latin. Or was it French?

'Like a prune,' said Lottie, 'I can just picture her.'

Francis started to doze off as he thought of Vera. Maybe he would call into the pub again, maybe he could just chat to her, no harm at all in conversation and she was a fine looking woman. Lottie took away the tray and carried it downstairs. The night was quiet. She left the tray on the kitchen sink, not feeling like washing up.

'I'll do that tomorrow,' she said, feeling quite pleased with herself. Who was it that was always putting things off till tomorrow?

Was it Scarlett O'Hara in *Gone with the Wind*? That was one of her favourite films. She remembered the night she saw it with Francis. There was even an intermission. He bought her a bottle of orange and some sweets. She wished she had that time back now.

Like a prune, thought Lottie as she went upstairs to bed. No shame. Drinking alone, she muttered to herself as she rubbed in her Ponds cold cream.

The Lake District, that would be nice. She'd buy some sensible blouses in Marks & Spencer's and get her hair done a few weeks beforehand. It would be just perfect for the trip. They could eat out. They'd have some walks and in the evenings she'd be able to watch *Emmerdale* and Coronation Street in the fancy televisions they always had in these places. Did they call them plastic or something? Or was it plasma?

They wouldn't have RTE of course but Alice, her next door neighbour, could tape the few episodes of *Fair City* she'd miss. It would only be six or seven so that would be no problem to Alice.

Meanwhile in another corner of the city in a larger room, Vera Bradbury turned off her bedside lamp. She knew she'd lie awake again as she had most nights for the past twelve months since she'd lost her husband. That didn't bother her. She was used to it.

She'd had a good night. She'd met a man who could discuss books, even books written by someone not many people knew about, like Thomas Hardy.

Francis was s a cultured man, He was a handsome and a decent man and Vera thought you could do a whole lot worse. She'd probably drop into that pub again. Perhaps on the same evening as she had before. She might even mention the book club in the library.

It would be nice to have a man to bring along, someone who shared her interest in reading. Yes, she would do that. She'd tell him about it next week.

# TREES

It's often said that lovers growing old together resemble one other in appearance. The reasons given for this strange fact are a sharing of moods of joy and sorrow, the constant watching of each other's expressions. And of course love.

Lately, I think I look like trees. Trees that you see these winter days – barren, gaunt, withered trees. I'm getting old and wizendish myself and often I hear myself say catty and barren things.

I usually divide them into two categories: Fairview Park/St. Stephen's Green Group and Lonesome Corporation Planted On Our Avenue Group. I look like the latter and I love them best of all.

Fairview Park trees rattle at the window of the bus every morning as I pass by. They're tall and willowy and wave and weave like ladies of the ballet. St. Stephen's Green Over By The Duck Pond Trees are like fancy dames in the Gresham Hotel. They crane their long necks and stand on tippy-toes on their six-inch heels trying to get a glimpse of their reflections under the soft flattering street  lights and push and jostle as they seek to admire their own beauty.

They get tangled up in each other just like the leafy trees, each one so involved in admiring their own sad-eyed images.  They smell of exotic perfumes, their puffed-out faces staring back at them as they try to pull their swollen lips into the semblance of a smile. They're oh-so-polite and make false comments to each other, remarking on designer clothes and shoes, meanwhile thinking that they themselves are so much more beautiful than anything around them. 'Who let her out?' they think of their rivals, 'That tree should be locked up.' The rings of cellulite lie hidden under their expensive garments, revealing their ages just like the rings on the trunks of the summer trees tell us they're as old as time.

Once upon a time I loved trees in spring. Pink trees with cherry blossoms brushed silently at the window of the No. 42 bus. Our avenue burst into bloom and I sang alleluia to Dublin Corporation for their nice present. Walking in St. Stephen's Green beside the statue of Wolfe Tone I saw birds making nests. I dreamed of my mate and myself rushing hither and thither - to building societies and bank managers, I suppose – to furnish our love nest. In my dreams the mundane was covered in exotic wrappings. I wandered through a smoky blue haze of lace and saucepans, hen parties and confetti, Rimini and Ranelagh, 'Pork chops for two, please,' and never being alone again. Each spring I dreamed like that, once upon a time.

Some while ago I fell in love with autumn trees. Maybe not so much with the trees as the leaves they were losing. I was happy plodding along beside them. I cocked my ear to the rustling music they made. Sniffing it reminded me of Sunday morning rashers. Men in uniforms swept leaves of red and green and yellow and brown into mounds and when no one was looking in I'd leap in among them and have leaves up to my knees.

I had a dream about those leaves and this is it. Like a thief I'd creep up behind Wolfe Tone's hard and stony statue  and plant some sticks of gelignite under him. Then I'd explode them and he'd soar over the Shelbourne Hotel and in his hurry wouldn't he forget his high boots. Quick as lightning I'd abandon my shoes and tights and jump into his stone boots. They'd probably be icy cold against my legs and maybe I'd have bloody toes from chips of stone but I'd still dance into Stephen's Green.

I'd gather up every single solitary leaf and roll them together into a ginormous multi-coloured crackling football. By the time I'd kicked my way to Grafton Street all of Dublin would be out to see what was causing the crashing noise stone boots would make when they met a leafy football. Loud shrieks would come from shop girls, bank clerks, waitresses, hairdressers apprentices, pensioners, paper boys, beauticians, models in training, massagers of excess weight and  smartly dressed  ladies from  travel agents  who'd down tools and jauntily place their biros behind lonely pink ears, leaving K. Ziggheimmer from Ontario to write his own ticket.

Leaves would cling to hair. Sad varicose-veined legs would be hidden inside thick elastic tights , necks, ears, eyes, throats, bony knees and battered bruised hearts. The bald heads of lonesome lean poets would be lost inside bodies of old fat disillusioned men. Some serious people would stop and stare and listen to the explanation of a professor from Trinity College who'd talk about a form of madness due to frustration, vaguely reminiscent of the peasant march in Tibet when people of that region left work benches to play when granny lost her needle one day in spring.

Streams of my leafy football would blow over O'Connell Bridge and float down the mucky Liffey. A typist would say to some Chartered Accountant as the 42A turned at the Custom House, 'Would you look at the leaves in the Liffey.' But he wouldn't hear her, his mind being concentrated on Capital Expenditure and Debtors Balance Sheets.

Mr. Daniel O'Connell, meanwhile, would receive me with open arms in O'Connell Street and personally escort me to my throne. Of course you can expect the three stone hussies around him would start whining. 'Where will our Josie sit when she comes back from her gall bladder operation?' But Daniel would soon put a stop to them. They'd be jealous of my thin arms, them with their fat flabby things all riddled with vaccination marks they pretended were bullet holes.

I'd stay with Daniel for ever and ever and sometimes we'd pass the time playing I spy with my little eye something beginning with A – A for Ants. That would be people  scurrying and hurrying to the G.P.O. Then B for Bats. That would be the ones running to catch their pension, afraid they wouldn't make it quick enough to the grave. Then C, D, E, F, G until we got to H. H would be for Happy Daniel because that's what he'd be. Me too. Because I'd always have the smell of autumn with me.

Nowadays I love winter trees. I love them when brown hair is washed and drops drip down drooping onto necks and narrow shoulders. I love them when Mother uses a fine comb to trap nits picked up from dirty school pals and you can see the sky through the many partings. I love them all dolled up for a dance, their beautiful bodies naked to the world. And I love them best on our avenue.

I suppose I'm getting old. Maybe in a short time now I'll have no more dreams of my mate or building love nests, no plans for blowing up Wolfe Tone just to borrow his boots. Winter Barren Trees: I am, indeed, the living image of you.

Sometimes I watch you all from my window and you give me a nod. I know then that you know that I'm not one bit pushed really that all the rest of the women on the avenue are married even though sometimes I'm a little cold and lonely on top of my electric blanket.

I understand that you're glad to be on our avenue but sometimes I know you long to sway with the wind in Fairview Park. Maybe one of these days you'll dickey up and tog yourself out in spring finery and desert me. Who will I have then? I'll be an old maid telling myself, 'All that colour is vulgar anyway,' while all the time inside envying you your youth.

Spring and winter, autumn and summer: which trees are best? Maybe you summer ones aren't all stuck-up bitches after all. Thinking of you from afar you seem like strapping big woman far removed from barren skinny hags. Maybe you can teach me to enjoy myself. Maybe you and I could become acquainted. Maybe if I studied your moods and watched your expressions love would follow. Maybe I could get to resemble you in appearance after a time. Maybe I could yet blossom into a vision of mature womanhood.

That's what I'll do with myself, fall in love with the summer trees. If I started preparing myself with warm smiles and gentle phrases I'd be ready to strike up a relationship with them by about July. Surely those lovely ladies can break into the cynical person that is now my mind. Surely those buxom belles can make me laugh again.

Maybe they'll become my friends. Maybe I'm not that desolate. Maybe there's yet hope for a lonely old tree-watcher like me.

# SOME CRAZY MIXED-UP BIRD

On Friday morning your woman from Artane lay in her bed staring up at a winding crack on the ceiling. She composed speeches to Margo Murphy who once lived next door and was now married and residing south of the river. She thought she might one day write these speeches in a letter. She might even call them out over the phone. It was almost certain they'd never leave her mind.

They were her way of getting rid of the anger she felt at the snobbery of others. They concerned her feelings about people's hearts being broken. People who'd walked the feet off themselves in Killarney town to purchase presents for their two grandchildren.

An Aran jumper which cost a fortune for little Lisa and a sailor suit with a peaked cap for baby Matthew.   A jolly leprechaun swinging out of a lamp-post and a little thatched cottage with 'Welcome to Killarney' on its hall door for their ignorant daughter and her cold fish of a husband.

All of these gifts were thrown into a plastic bag for the bin men to collect on Friday morning along with bits and pieces of rubbish, totally unsuitable for a double income home in Stillorgan.

Her latest missive to Margot Murphy (now Margaret Duffy O'Byrne) read:

*'Believe me, I know the situation. I do understand how very full and demanding your life is.  Our last get-together for a drink and a chat was most stimulating. I appreciate your need to be honest and I know that in the whole sphere of life the handing out of cheap knick-knacks is totally irrelevant. Your mother stopped me again yesterday to ask if I'd heard from you. Your dad looks thinner but that's not my business. They never had lectures on how to relate, Margot; presenting presents is their way of communicating love. There's no need to stuff your conclusions down tired old throats. Leave them their 1916. Spare them the real truth about dead heroes and let them keep their rosary. If the development of one's potential and*

*fulfilment is what you're after I'm glad I'm illogical and perhaps even dishonest. So for God's sake, Margot, pretend. Call over to Artane and bring the nippers and then worship Buddha and discuss the thinking woman's reading of the term 'charity' for the rest of your life.'*

End of speech to the girl next door, now married.

She then went on to address her boyfriend.

*'Dear Cute Cautious Citizen,*

*Sometimes you remind me of an alcoholic who recently joined A.A. for the 29<sup>th</sup> time. Sneaky and cunning, he keeps the evil bottle locked in a press. Now and again he permits himself a peek to make sure the mixture is still available. Now and again he sinks to rock bottom and takes a swig of the stuff, but the loss of freedom, the dependence on one bottle for enjoyment (when the earth abounds with so many bottles), causes him to loathe himself. And so our big-time lover locks up the bottle, carefully pockets the key and stays away – until the next time. Falling in love suits you all right. Take three gleeful somersaults in the air and dive in. I love you, come on, take my hand.'*

End of imaginary conversation with her love.

Suddenly the crack in the ceiling split open and up went your woman from the bed out through the roof and far above Artane until children dribbling along to Killester School were no more than dots.

She found herself seated on a brown feathery cushion. When she took a look down at her foot, size six and a half, she saw it was now the size of a little speck of sleep you'd take from your eye. She was perched on the back of a sparrow and the sparrow was, in relation to herself, roughly the size of an elephant.

'Mammy, Daddy!' she screamed, 'Help! What's happening/ Am I out of my mind?'

Whereupon the sparrow, who wore wellingtons, said, 'Less of the screeching, young one. It's no ball game for me either. Stop pulling out of me scarf or you'll choke me.'

'But where am I? Is this the nuthouse?'

'No,' said the sparrow. He stared at her sourly. She saw he had a deep cleft in his chin and wore goggles.

'No, you're not in any nuthouse. We leave such places for the final step in evolution. The fully developed human being, shall we say. The *crème de la crème,* so to speak. The leaders and the followers; the micksers and the mollyers; the spinsters and the ministers; the homely, the glamorous, the sophisticated and the amorous and of course the dames in love. We mustn't forget those lassics. We leave the nuthouse for that shower. Plus the bags, the hags and all other assortments of humanity in this fine world of ours. We sparrows don't lose our minds because we haven't such articles to lose. Neither do we suffer from our nerves.

Your woman was gobgasted and flabbersmacked.

'Tell me this and tell me no more,' the sparrow went on, 'Did you ever hear the expression 'birdbrain'? It's used by your race when one party wishes to insult the other's intelligence. Well, okay, our brains are indeed small, but this in keeping with our small heads. What we lack in size we make up for in our good sense. And, of course, our class.'

'We used to call a woman in Galway 'Sparrow legs',' said your woman, giving a wild raucous laugh out of her.

'My point exactly,' said the sparrow, 'You insult their legs by comparing them to birds and as already mentioned their brains, same story. . Don't you also insult the female of the species by using the term 'birds' to describe them?'

'We do, for sure. What's it to you?'

'A lot, I daresay. And furthermore, tell me this. What's the matter with *my* two pins? Look at them, will you? There now. Neat, shapely, and not a trace of a varicose vein. When I do the foxtrot or the Siege of Ennis I'm no mean tomato.'

You could have knocked your woman over with a fender.

'Are you in love?' she asked the sparrow when she recovered her composure.

'I'm married, if you must know,' said the sparrow. 'My mate's name is Gertrude. She's a dab hand at frying a worm and keeping a nest neat and tidy.'

'Is that all she means to you?'

'I don't get you. What are you talking about?'

'You said she keeps the nest neat and tidy as if that was the most important thing to you.'

'I help her whenever I can. We look after each other. Are you happy now?'

'What I'm trying to get at is, how do you relate to her?'

'What's that supposed to mean?'

'What I'm saying is, can she develop her personality within the confines of the nest. In other words, is your wife no more than hired help?"

'Hired help? Not on your nelly. No, Gertie is for keeps. We don't go in for that divorce lark like you humans.'

'You sound a bit too sure of yourself.'

'If I am, it's with good reason. Gertie is happy. We have two babies and are expecting a third after Christmas. We're a lovely family. Each one contributes his or her own part – his or her own unique part – to the good of that family.'

'Unique!' said your woman. 'That really slays me. There are billions of your kind on the go. Brown fellows, all exactly the same. Unique? Don't make me laugh.'

'Shut your face, you hussy,' said the sparrow, 'or I'll shut it for you. Was it one developed human being the Good Lord said would not fall without His knowing of it? No, it was one *sparrow*. The Lord had His priorities right but you're falling, and falling fast. You're going to finish yourselves off with your shooting of bodies and your crippling of minds, with your stresses and ambitions and your stupidity. We shall yet inherit the earth, we humble sparrows, as well as my friends the starlings, robins and hens. And by the way, that was a low trick you played on our cousins the hens. What did you hope to achieve by that lie?'

'What lie?' said your woman.

'I'll tell you what lie. You locked the poor creatures up so you did. You shone electric lights on them, codding them into thinking there was no such a thing as night. You had them laying eggs like blazes so you could fill your greedy bellies with all kinds of delicacies. Well, Miss, the hens now know what you were up to and they'll get you back.'

'How do they know?' said your woman.

'We told them,' said the sparrow.

'Spoilsport,' said your woman.

'That's a good one,' said the sparrow. 'I must say I like your definition of sport. It shows a real understanding of philosophy. The strong take over weak, isn't that it? And then you continue to use your strength for your own greedy desires. Typical "human" attitude, that.'

'So how are the hens going to get us back?'

'Oh, I don't know. Maybe they won't bother. Maybe they'll leave revenge to you lot.'

'You don't have much respect for human beings, do you?'

'No, I'm afraid. How could I respect young ones who won't even visit their parents and shove presents from Killarney town into black plastic bags?'

'That's below the belt,' said your woman. That was an isolated incident.'

'It's happening all over', said the sparrow, 'and what's sauce for the goose is sauce for the gander. Speaking of ganders, will you have a gander at yourself? You're not doing so hot with that male friend of yours, are you? It's not exactly love's young dream.'

'How did you know about that?'

'A little bird told me – excuse the pun.'

'He has to find himself,' said your woman.

'Well, thirty nine years is a hell of a time to be looking.'

'Watch your sarcasm. Marriage is a big step. He has to be sure.'

'Get up the yard,' said the sparrow. 'You'd be mighty glad to take him, sure or not. He'll probably get sure when he's about ninety-five and a half.'

Whereupon your woman from Artane caught the two tails of the sparrow's scarf and in a frenzy pulled them tight. The sparrow then dropped from the heavens with your woman hanging on to his little legs.

He looked to be set for destruction but then God put out His hand and, neatly removing your woman, He cast her into the ocean.

The sparrow He stroked and gently kissed with the kiss of life and sent him off home to Gertie and the kids.

That evening they all dined on roasted earwig smothered in mayonnaise.

# THE ANNIVERSARY

When our relationship was six months old I bought a shiny yellow raincoat to celebrate. Mammy thought it was lovely. She admired me going out in it.

As I walked along to the place we were to meet I felt funny noises in my stomach. The noises were squissshhhing and guggaling and going leeeeunka as they tried to break down the elasticated barrier of my strong supporting panties and splay themselves all over the pavement.

My knees and toes were imprisoned by the double mesh of my tights and the stiff leather wrapping of my new black boots. They writhed and rattled and begged to be released so they could shoot out and dance and bound around the town in abandoned gaiety.

It was February.

Going home from work on the bus earlier, the cold month oozed from overcoats. February seeped through newspapers and slid down windows. February frowned as a frozen frigid faceful of grey mist threw itself at all of us people on the bus.

And then.

*And then.*

In the time it took to have my tea and get ready…yes, *in the time it took to have my tea and get ready,* … Dublin had sailed away into September.,

I could smell it and taste it. I saturated myself in its yellow glow as I went in my yellow coat to meet my love,

I saw myself in a shop window and I was like some other girl. Some girl in a magazine story dreaming of marriage. I thought there'd soon be a watch or charm bracelet, soon a diamond ring and soon Torremolinos, followed by a Terenure semi-d, hen parties, canteens of cutlery and never being alone again.

Up the street two travellers, a woman and a man were fighting, .
The woman had something in her arms.

The man was waving a bottle high above his head like a discus
thrower. As I walked by them the woman dropped the bundle she
was carrying and darted down the street with the man close behind
her. The bundle opened its mouth and started to roar. It was a baby,
a tinty strap of humanity.

I walked on. It was only five minutes until our meeting and he
liked me to be punctual.

The little baby screamed louder; I turned back and leaned down
to it. Its face was dirty and it had a stale smell. I picked it up and
held it close. I suppose it was my maternal instinct or something but
I wished I could take it home and keep it with me forever.

I wanted to wash it in a huge big tub and powder it and then to
dress it up in soft pretty clothes. I saw myself walking it out in one
of those high prams with the lovely fringe hoods. As I cradled it I
whispered the stupid things fat old dames whisper to babies. It must
have worked though because it stopped it crying. It seemed to be
contented in my arms.

I must have been some time dreaming because when I came back
to reality a crowd had gathered.

'They're getting better dressed every day,' said a woman in an
expensive leather coat. .

'It's the system I blame,' said a man.

'Hey you – where did you get the child?' said a scruffy young
fella.

I wanted to drop the baby and run but they'd built a solid wall
round me. I felt incapable of doing anything.

'It's the system, so it is,' said the man once more. He was small
and fat with a very red face.

'What system?' said a serious-looking young fella.

'The system, the political system, Red Face explained.

'There's *no* system, that's what's wrong,' said the young man.

They looked at the baby.

'It's not mine,' I whispered.

'She's well able to dress herself, mind you,' said Leather Coat, in her posh southside drawl.

'That's just it,' said the young man, 'Single mothers living off the government on my hard-earned taxes.'

'Give us a euro,' said the scruffy little boy.

'Go away,' I told him.

'Shame on you, you're unfit to have children' someone in crowd shouted.

'The Irish are a dirty nation,' said the serious young man. ''They breed children like rabbits and then have no conception of basic hygiene. The Swedes are the only race who know about cleanliness. Give me the Swedes every time.'

'It's the system, the system,' screamed Red Face.

And then at the back of the crowd I saw him.

'Len,' I called, 'Len.' But he'd crossed the street. He seemed not to hear me.

'Here's more of them,' said Red Face.

The traveller woman was pushing her way through the crowd like a mad thing. Everyone stood back frightened by her savage emotion. Her mouth was bleeding. I was afraid she was going to hit me.

'Ah Miss,' she said, 'Thanks for minding John Joe.'

She took the baby to her and suddenly I felt superfluous and in the way.

'Come on, Hannah,' said the man, who was weaving his way towards her. He was minus his bottle. They walked away. She clutching the baby he with one arm around her waist.

It was then I felt the wetness.

'Hey, Miss,' said the scruffy little young fella, 'The baby pissed on your coat, Miss. Go on, give us a euro.'

The crowd dispersed. I saw Len crossing the street and called him but he didn't answer. I went over to meet him.

He was, as always, his perfect self, having very good taste in clothes.

'Why didn't you come when I called you?' I asked.

'I'm not exactly fond of making an exhibition of myself. What, might I ask, were you doing with the baby?' He didn't say anything about my new coat.

'The mother and father were fighting. She was running away from him. She left the baby on the footpath,'

'So what? What's that to do with you?'

'It's only tiny. I couldn't leave it there. The poor little thing was frozen.'

'That's none of your business. Those types are always fighting. Permanently drunk if you ask me. You know what they say about what to do when you see two travellers fighting.'

'What do they say?'

'Never involve yourself because in the end they'll turn on you. That's the kind they are.'

'Don't generalise. Everyone is different.'

'No they're not. All those knackers are trouble. I could tell you stories.'

'I don't want to hear them.'

'Anyway, where would you like to go?'

Already the magic of the evening was gone.

'I don't know. I'm not pushed.'

'We have three choices' he said, 'A drink, a film or a coffee.'

'Let's just go for a walk.'

'You must be joking. It's too cold for that.'

'I think it's a lovely evening, Len.  Just like autumn.'

'Oh yeah.  Right.  Autumn in February. Totally normal. What happened to your coat, by the way? Is it a different one than you usually have?

'It is. The baby wet it. Do you like it?'

'Jesus, you're mad. Do I like a coat with piss on it.'

'There's no need to be so snotty.'

'Come on,' he said, 'We'll go the pictures.'

He started to walk and I shuffled along behind him reluctantly. I was happy to have helped the little baby but now John Joe was ruining our date. I tried to get the smell off my coat but I couldn't

After a few minutes we got to the cinema. Len bought two tickets. I didn't even look to see what was on.

It was dark inside. I tripped on the stairs the way you do after going from light to darkness. Len said, 'Are you blind or something? You'll have me disgraced. People will think you're drunk.'

I took off my coat and put it on a seat beside me so Len wouldn't have to smell it.

Images flashed before my eyes without me even being aware of them. There was a 'few trailers on first.  Then some ads.

Len put his arm around me. That was a big deal for him. He wasn't usually demonstrative.

Then the film started. It was a drama of some sort. There was lots of talking and no action. He kept his arm around me all through it. I was uncomfortable not being able to move but I didn't like to tell him because he usually got into bad form if you said things like that.

The film ended and we got up out of our seats. Len stretched and yawned as we walked towards  the exit.

Outside I still thought the weather seemed strange. It was like autumn.

'Look, Len,' I said, 'Can't you smell it?

'Smell what?'

'September.'

'Are you mad? It's spring and a lousy typical Irish spring.. Did you enjoy the film?'

'It was okay but I want to know if you can smell the air. That's what I love about this country. You never know what the weather is going to do. As they say, you get the four seasons in one day.'

'If you ask me,' he said, 'We get winter all the year round in this dump.'

There was no point in talking to him so we just walked on. He was probably thinking about the film. I was hoping the baby smell was gone from my coat.

We passed by a park. I got a sudden urge to jump around in it.

'Hey, Len, let's see if we can get into the park,' I said.

'How could we? It's closed.'

'We could hop over the railings. Nobody would see us. Come on, Len. For the crack.'

'I'm climbing over no railings. Get a grip, will you? We haven't the time, anyway. If you want to get your bus you better hurry.'

'Forget the bus, I feel drunk tonight. It's our anniversary.'

'Anniversary? Of what?'

Men never remembered things like that.

'All right, forget it. Just let's do something. It seems flat just going home.'

'Look, we have exactly 45 minutes before your bus comes. That means just enough time for a quick – and I mean quick - coffee.'

There was a restaurant nearby, the one we usually went to with the sign hanging off and the pink tablecloth. We went over to it and sat down. Len ordered coffee for two and two scones without asking me what I wanted. We always had that but tonight I wanted something different.

I took off my coat and sat down. Len kept his on. We were sitting opposite each other. He looked strange to me. I think he had a new jacket on. His shirt was buttoned all the way up to the top. He always did that in cold weather. I imagined him getting ready to meet me, the effort he must have had to do himself up.

'How is the job going?' I said. He was studying to be a solicitor.

'I had a rough day so I'd prefer to forget it if you don't mind.'

'Go on, tell me. Tell me about the, what do you call it, conveyancing stuff.'

'Some other time. Anyway it's too technical for you.'

Instead he started giving out to me about the way I'd behaved with the baby, making a disgrace of myself. Then he went into all the other things he didn't like about me. I could have got mad but I wasn't really listening to him. I was too busy looking out at the golden night.

'Look, the time is racing by,' he said after a while, 'We better go. I'd hate you to miss your bus. A taxi costs a fortune. Are you ready?'

'Yes I'm ready.'

He paid the waitress and left a small tip on the table.

I put on my coat. I was wondering if he still got the smell.

We walked to the bus in silence.

'Thanks for the film,' I said.

'Don't mention it,' Len said, 'It's a pity you didn't like it more.'

'It wasn't too bad.'

The bus swung around the corner. It screeched to a halt and I got on. I thought he might kiss me before it started moving again but he didn't.

'Well I'll give you a ring,' he said, tipping me on the arm.

'Great, I'll look forward to it.'

I sat on the bus and watched him walk up the quays. He seemed very small as the bus drove on. He didn't wave or look back.

He didn't say when he was going to ring, I thought, as we gathered speed. He always gave a day but this time he didn't. Would he bother ringing me at all?

At the back of the bus a couple were wrapped around each other. They were like the pair from the film *Basic Instinct* where she was the killer. Len was more like Clark Gable in *Gone with the Wind*: 'Frankly my dear, I don't give a damn.'

He didn't say when.

He didn't say when.

I kept saying that to myself. It was beating out a rhythm in my head.

Len didn't kiss me at the film. He didn't even kiss me when we parted. It was our anniversary but he didn't admire my new yellow coat.

He didn't say when,

He didn't say when.

The bus drove on as I beat the drum of Len in my mind. Then it came to a stop, My stop.

I got off. I walked up the road thinking of Clark Gable and Len and our six months together. My stomach was still guggalling, but for different reasons now.

He didn't say when.

He didn't say when.

After I got to the house I went straight upstairs to my room. Mammy was already asleep. I heard her snoring coming from the front bedroom.

It was cold when I took off my clothes. I fell asleep thinking of the trees shedding their leaves and the cold moon dipped down behind a cloud.

I had strange dreams, dreams of wild animals and rolling fields and lying in the rain. Len was beside me for some of them and then he wasn't.

Then morning came

As I drew back the curtains I saw the cold grey dreary February day. It looked starved of sunshine. Starved, a funny word. Like we used to starve ourselves of sweets and treats in Lents gone by.

Where were my clothes? I found my tights with their r guts spilt out all over a chair. I didn't feel like putting them on but I did, managing to pull the large tear up above my knees. My boots were sagging near the bed. Under the eiderdown my support panties were wheezing and gasping their last.

I went downstairs.   Mammy was in the kitchen buttering toast.

'How did last night go?' she asked me.

'Okay,' I answered, 'It was our anniversary.'

'Anniversary?' said Mammy, 'Of what?'

'Of six months going out.'

'Six months? That's a funny kind of anniversary.'

'Maybe I'm a funny kind of girl.'

I finished my breakfast. Mammy was looking at me kind of funny. I got up and put on my old brown coat.

Mammy came out from the kitchen.

'Do you think he's serious about  you?' she asked..

'No.'

I had to be honest.

Mammy looked upset.

'Ah, that's a pity, I know you like him.'

'Don't worry about me,' I said, 'I'm tough.'

# EXPERIENCE 181

Experience. A great word of mine. I use it in all my conversations with myself. It describes all the happenings that cause me either tears or wild joyous mirth. Most of these, I should add, take place in my mind. Every few days I travel to outer space or to the outer reaches of Mongolia with Mills & Boon type of men on white chargers who take me to their tents and make passionate love to me.

At other times, when I give my mind the day off, I write letters to people I fancy. I wrote one to an actor once. He was Patsy O'Connor, the main star in a TV show I used to watch called *Down on the Farm*. He played a character called Dano, the local vet. He looked my type, so masculine helping mother cows to give birth to little calves or injecting fluffy sheep to spare them from worms and fluke and all kind of horrors. I wasn't sure how to word the letter so I copied it from one some famous person wrote centuries ago. It could have been Virgil or one of those Roman fellas.

*Down on the Farm* was a soap. It went out on Tuesdays and Thursdays from half seven to eight. In the series Dano wore a tweed jacket with leather patches and corduroy pants. His hair was greying at the temples and he had a crumpled academic look. Vets are like doctors, their mission in life being to help the afflicted. Just my type of fella.

My letter was about a man seeing a woman after a long absence, a woman he loved dearly. 'A burning flame devours me,' it said, 'There's not a drop of blood within me that doesn't tingle. I recognise the signals of an ancient flame. Without you my life has no meaning.'

The letter seemed quite beautiful to me at the time. It was passionate and so intellectual. My dreams at that time were of someday meeting an intellectual. I saw teachers and vets as intellectuals then. Maybe they still are. I mean, all that study and application. At the end of my missive I put in brackets: 'If you wish to light this flame, please attend The Sliver Slipper Club, Portmarnock on Friday, 24<sup>th</sup> September *circa* 11 p.m.' That was a place we used to go dancing.

I put a line under the word *circa* to indicate that I knew it was foreign. I knew Virgil would have liked that, whatever about Dano. At the end I wrote, 'I will be sitting at the table in corner on the balcony. The one just beside the bar. Signed, Miss X.' And I posted it off. About five minutes later I wanted to put my hand back down the letterbox so I could tear it up. I convinced myself I'd just made the biggest mistake of my life, bar none.

Friday came. In the early part of the night I went out for a few drinks with Tessa Flanagan. Tessa is my best friend. She wanted to go to a club in Terenure but my mind was on the letter. I got this Big Thing that I had to go and see Dano. I'm always like that. One minute I'll tell myself the last place on earth is to be with a certain gentleman and the next I'll come to the conclusion that my life will be a total failure if I don't see him. It gets confusing for Tessa. I had a job persuading her but eventually she agreed to come to the Silver Slipper with me.

We got a taxi out, which she grumbled about. I felt if I was going to meet a legend arriving by bus just wasn't on.

When we were half way there I told her about the famous letter. (I forgot to mention I have a mouth as big as the Shannon).

'You bloody eejit,' she said, 'He's a nobody. What possessed you?' I didn't know. I couldn't explain it.

'Look,' I said, 'What's done is done. It is what it is. Let's make the best of it.' She threw her eyes to heaven.

'If you ever do anything like this again,' she told me, 'I'll disown you.' I promised I wouldn't.

It was about half past ten when we got to the dance. Tessa made a bee-line for the Ladies but I didn't bother. One thing I've learnt from dances is: Don't go to the Ladies until you're well settled into the night. It destroys the whole night. You can look like a rose in your own bathroom or in the soft glow from a pub toilet mirror but in the Ladies of a dance-hall you can wilt and wane like a faded, jaded pissy-bed. It's to do with competition. Surrounded by lilies from Lucan, roses from Rialto, carnations from Cabra and dahlias from Drumcondra, your confidence disappears. Which is fatal in a club for mingling and meeting the opposite sex, men liking confidence and all that.

As soon as we got inside I saw him. There he was in a cravat and the tweed jacket and beige trousers, perched at a table on the balcony. He was sitting with a fellow who plays the headmaster in the programme. Even though he was sitting down I could see he was tiny. The teeth also looked a bit too much like piano keys to be real. And was that wig on his head? It looked far too tidy to be actual hair.

I thought to myself: What have you got yourself into? He was trying to look nonchalant but you could see he was watching the door and checking his watch. Waiting for Burning Fire to come sizzling in, no doubt.

Anyway, cool as you please I went to the upstairs bar. I got myself a dry martini and a vodka for Tessa. When she came out of the Ladies I decided I'd ask your man Dano for his autograph. Just for the gas.

It so happened Tessa thought the other fellow might be interesting. She was all on to make contact with him so she kept nagging at me to go over.

'Go on,' she said, 'the headmaster fellow is only gorgeous.' I couldn't agree. To me he looked just like a shrivelled-up prawn, pink and slimy.

'All right,' I said as if it didn't matter too much to me one way or the other. So I went over to them.

The minute I said 'Excuse me,' the TV star literally sparkled. Did he know already that I was Burning Fire?

'Can I have your autograph?' I asked him, stuttering the words out like a crazy teenager.

'Certainly you can have my autograph', he said, 'certainly, my love. But won't you and your friend join us? What are you drinking?'

Well, talk about turning on the charm. He couldn't do enough for us. Prawnface couldn't take his eyes off Tessa. Tessa gets that all the time. Probably because she acts like she doesn't care. Ladies Toilets or any of my other complexes don't daunt Tessa. She just bursts with confidence.

Prawnface was watching her like he'd just come through the Gobi Desert and hadn't seen a woman for nine years. And Tessa is womanhood personified. She has curves in places where I don't even have places. But Dano was concentrating on Burning Fire. He kept fixing his cravat and giving me these cheesy smiles.

The next few minutes are hazy to me. Tessa disappears into the place where Prawnface is sitting and Words Are Exchanged. I'm not sure what kinds of words but I deduced they weren't about the weather. Tessa moves fast in things like that and Prawnface looked like he didn't need much encouragement.

Then the pair of them got up to dance. Suddenly I found myself alone with Dano..

'What's your name, love?' he asked me.

'Rachel,' I said.

This was a big lie of course but I felt Rachel was suited to Burning Fire for some reason. (Maybe Scarlet would have been better).

'Rachel. A very nice name. And where do you hail from, Ravishing Rachel? Heaven? Or is it perhaps hell? You certainly look hot, hot and fiery.'

After that he gave a snort. Talk about subtle. Suddenly I decided I hated him. He had piggy eyes like one of the livestock in the series. Maybe he got them from looking at pigs all day long.

Anything was possible. Monkey see, monkey do. Or piggy see, piggy do.

'Don't be shy,' he said, 'Come on, let's dance.' He had this put-on accent, not a bit like Dano. How could I ever trust my television ever again?

It so happened it was a slow dance. Just my luck. I had mouthfuls of his hair twisted round my windpipe. Talk about smothering yourself with the kind of after-shave men who think of themselves as Men use.

'Relax,' he whispered. 'Ease out, love. Don't be frightened.'

I decided that if it came to the push and if he stood over me with a dagger. I was going to swear blind I never wrote that letter. All I wanted was to find Tessa and get home.

'I'm not frightened,' I muttered, moving away from him.

Obviously he realised I'd lost my nerve. The confrontation with him in the flesh had reduced me to an imbecile.

'Where's Tessa?' I said.

'Come now, we'll have another drink. Tessa will be all right. Jimmy will look after her.'

'I want to talk to her.'

'Later. Come on, we'll just sit here and get to know each other a bit better.' With that he gives another insinuating snort. Me, I stare blankly ahead as if I don't notice a thing.

He went up to the counter and waltzed back a few minutes later with some drinks in tow. He must have got me a double martini because it looked huge.

'I need to wind down from the alcohol,' I said. 'Maybe we should just have two glasses of water or something. How about a glass of milk?'

'Milk? Are you mad? Anyway I'm lactose intolerant.'

Lactose intolerant? That was a new one on me. I didn't even know what it meant. I was suddenly starting to feel Dano intolerant.

'Okay,' I said, 'I'll have the martini, but only because it's there.'

'That's my girl. That's why they climbed Mount Everest, wasn't it? Because it was there. It's not a bad reason.'

It was like drinking vinegar to me. My stomach wasn't ready for it. It was shouting 'No!' at me. But I wasn't listening.

After I swallowed the martini I felt a bit weird. We sat there looking at each other like daws. I hadn't the a clue what to say to him.

'You write with feeling,' he said.

'What?' I said as if I didn't know what he was on about.

'Your letter, I liked it.'

I didn't say a word to this. I thought I was being smart but I wasn't. I was giving myself away by my silence.

'It was so assertive. So, how shall I put it, direct and poetical. But now you seem like such a quiet little thing. Relax. Ease out, Rachel. Do you know you have lovely eyes? Eyes that give signals, if you get my meaning.'

He started blathering about his career, how people thought it was all glamour being a TV star. You'd imagine he was Brad Pitt the way he was talking.

'We have to get up at all hours of the morning in all weathers,' he said, 'and say the same lines over and over again till we get them right.' I was thinking, 'A pity about you, you poor soul, that sounds worse than being one of the starving children in Biafra.' But all I said was, 'Oh my God, I never realised.' (The idiot didn't even know I was being sarky).

At this stage my burning fire was turning into a damp cinder. Maybe if he was on the *Late Late* or something he'd have got away with it but all I could do was stifle yawns. I was thinking: If I don't get out of here I'll just die. Or something worse.

He was getting sort of passionate. Exuding confidence, totally full up of himself. And all because of that stupid letter.

I looked him up and down again, now realising to my horror that his jacket wasn't tweed at all, just some gaudy-looking thing that didn't even go with the beige trousers. So much for actor's salaries. He was probably on the breadline. It was one other false thing about him to go with all the other false things. Maybe he *was* wearing a toupee as well. And false teeth.

'I must go to the Ladies,' I said, starting to burp, 'I think I've had a few too many. I may throw up.' How many times in my life had the Ladies rescued me from useless men? (They were much more important to me for that purpose than my bursting bladder).

My announcement put a stop to his gallop. He looked at me as if I'd vomited on him already. He obviously didn't want his cravat and his horrible pretendy tweed jacket covered with sick. Which just went to show the extent of his interest in Burning Fire.

I got myself into the Ladies. This time I really did throw up.

Not because of the martini, by the way, but the nerves. For this relief much thanks, as Shakespeare said. Or was it Tessa?

When I was finished my business I peeped out the door of the Ladies to see what Tessa was up to but she was nowhere to be seen. That left me and Dano – not a prospect to be relished.

I couldn't bear the thought of that scenario so I did a lousy thing. I got my coat and ducked out the back door without going back to Famous TV Star.

I went home in a taxi. All the way home I guilt-tripped myself.

Why did I go in the first place? Why did I leave? Why was I always biting off more than I could chew and then chewing it?

For good measure, after I got into the house I proceeded to throw up again. On my new carpet. Brilliant. Maybe I improved the colour of it.

After that I headed for the *leaba*. Who needed TV stars when you could cuddle up with a good book?

Except I couldn't concentrate on it. The guilt was still eating at me. I was also wondering how the bold Tessa got on with Prawnface.

Eventually I nodded off but after a while I heard some noise at the door.

It was Tessa coming in. She clumped up the stairs. In she came to the room looking the worse for wear.

'What happened?' she said accusingly.

'I had to leave,' I said, 'I got a panic attack.'

It wasn't too far from the truth. 'I noticed you got off with The Headmaster. At least one of us got something out of the night.' I was glad she had something to show for it after me dragging her out there and then abandoning her.

'That's a matter of opinion.'

'How do you mean?'

'Well let's put it like this. He wasn't exactly Paul Newman.'

'Did he make a pass at you?'

'If you call pawing me with what seemed like eight hands, yes.'

'How did Dano take my disappearing act?'

'He was like a bull. I suppose I could see his point. You started something and then you couldn't finish it. Not like Magnus Magnusson.'

'Who?' Tessa was always coming out with strange stuff like that.

'Never mind.'

'So Jimmy turned out to be a sex maniac.'

'He put Casanova in the shade. Tried to maul me every time we stopped at the lights he did. He was like a cannibal.'

That's what I like about Tessa. She calls a spade a spade.

'How did Dano take that?'

'Not very well. I could see him looking at us through the rear view mirror with daggers in his eyes. I could see him thinking it should have been him instead having Close Encounters of the 85th Kind with you.'

'You didn't respond to Prawnface's advances, did you?'

'Not likely. In fact I gave him a kick where it hurts.'

'Oh you didn't, Tessa.'

'Bloody right I did. And probably destroyed his marriage prospects into the bargain. It was the only way to stop him.'

'You're terrible.'

'*I'm* terrible? In case you've forgotten, sister, you got me into this mess. If it wasn't for you I'd have been at some club somewhere being chatted up by someone who didn't think he had the right to peel my clothes off just cos he was on the goggle-box.'

'So what happened then?'

'Prawnface took his beating and went off like a scalded cat clutching his family jewels. I had to resist a smile as I saw the poor lad disappearing into the night. He'll probably be off the series for a little while now. Maybe your fella will get more face time.'

'Did Dano drop you to the door?.'

'Yeah. He wanted to come in but I wouldn't let him. I knew he'd be upstairs to you like a shot to give out yards to you. I wanted to save you that. As it was, he spent about ten minutes at the door whinging about bitches and letters. Did you not hear him?'

'I must have been asleep. He's obviously a total crackpot. I can't get my head around that. He so intelligent on the telly.'

'Hello, he's an actor. They're all like that. Maybe that's the best acting they do – convincing us they're not as thick as the ditches they're living in.'

Tessa could be quite cruel when she wanted to, like someone else I know.

Me.

'Anyway,' she said, 'Will we go out for something to eat? I'm only starving.'

'Why not? If we rush out now the chipper will probably still be open.' It wouldn't have been the first midnight flit for us for some junk food to console us after yet another Lothario bit the dust.

So we did. We dined like lords on Big Macs, onion rings and a choccie milk shake each. On the way home we got ourselves a party pack of Taytos in the all-night supermarket for three euro. A steal! And slept like babies afterwards. (I've always found Taytos better than sleeping pills to help you sleep – and much more enjoyable to digest).

The next morning all we could do was laugh.

Wasn't life always like that? Things appeared huge when they were happening but became jokes 24 hours on.

But you now what? Even though it ended okay, it took me a while to recover from that little experience.

I know now I have to cop on to myself. Real life is different to what you see on the telly. That might sound obvious but it isn't. Especially if you're me.

I thought that was the end of the whole business but a few weeks later Dano rings me to get all the details of what happened to me on that fateful night.

I ask you, the neck of the man after the way I walked out on him. He must have got my phone number off Prawnface because it's the same as Tessa's one. You wouldn't need to be a genius to figure that out. I didn't think she'd have given it to him considering the way he pawed her. Maybe a part of her enjoyed it. You never know with Tessa.

'What about meeting for a cup of coffee?' he says then. I knew the cup of coffee I'd give him – right across his smacker.

'That sounds like a good idea,' I said, 'but not right now. An old flame has just come back into my life.' I always say that when I want to get rid of someone.

'An old flame,' he says, 'Hmm. More burning fires?'

'Who knows. Anyway, keep in touch. And continued success with the acting.'

'Thanks,' he says, 'Did I live up to your expectations from *Down on the Farm*?'

I nearly burst out laughing when he said that. All I could think of was him on all fours milking a cow in his wellies. I'm not as honest as Tessa so I didn't know how to reply.

'You look smaller than you do on the telly,' I blurted out.

He went quiet for a minute. Then he said, 'Really? What size is your telly?'

Smartarse.

# MOTHER AND CHILD

'Blessed are the paps that gave thee suck.'

That comes to my mind from some Bible things of years ago. In my day we didn't do much Bible. The Gospel according to St Luke we learnt off by heart and once I got first in the Bishops Exam. I failed my confirmation question but the bishop said, 'You're all right, I think you're a bit nervous.' He confirmed me anyway.

One girl heard me missing my question. I remember her name to this day. It was Angela Walsh. She promised never to let on to anyone and fair play to her she never did. I felt ashamed in my white pleated skirt and the fuzzy bolero my mother knitted. I always felt I'd fail for some reason or other, the same as I failed all my other exams, except for the Bishops Exam when I was in fourth class. In fact I feel a bit like that to this very day, that I'm already beaten before I start.

Anyway where was I? Oh yes, the paps. Think of paps like cows' udders.

'I have me udders,' a girl I knew always said when she had her period. Or at least it sounded like that. She meant 'My others.'

Udders. Fat and pink juicy things hanging down and little babies with their mouths pressed up against them for sustenance and warmth to make them fat healthy adults of sound mind, memory and understanding.

I wonder about my paps. Lonesome and sad at the years of waiting. 'The others' aren't as they used to be either. Tapering off to a trickle nowadays. Still and all, as I always say, that's life.

Did you ever get sick of yourself performing like a flea? You get sucked into things, like for instance being a secretary. Up with the lark and chained to my desk by nine on the dot. Reasonably tidy in appearance, although not completely top class, Heels worn down sometimes and the odd bit of egg or Tippex on the skirt. Still, without being too pernickety I get by.

And the paps lie silent through it all.

My mother is in a nursing home now. She's not young, but in comparison to the other people in there she is. Some of them sit sleeping all day and dutifully I go up and take their hands. I say a few words to the ones who are *compos mentis*, as we say in legal circles.

'How are you Gertie? How's things?'

'Marguerite, that's a lovely skirt.'

'Mary, did you get your hair done? It's only gorgeous.'

There are women from all walks of life in there. Retired ESB Officials and widows with nerve problems. One walks up and down all day, demented. Their paps are all out to grass now. Some of them have produced and given nourishment.

Sunday is visiting day. Packets of biscuits and pecks on the cheeks and the few kind words and then off with them with bags of mother's knickers for washing. Sad that. I think of nursing homes in Ballinasloe and Booterstown Drive with young ones taking care of old withered paps. Still you'd go mad all together if you let yourself think too much. No use complaining – though I do it anyway.

There are times I wonder about the busload of children I never had. I see them small and me a fat waddling hen of a woman with varicose veins and packets of disposable nappies hanging out of buggies.

In supermarkets in Clonsilla the shelves are laden down with nappies I never bought. Poor unclaimed nappies wilting away and me dreaming of sore bums that never saw the light of day or s nice dollop of sudocrem. I think of girls with plaits and Irish dancing medals and ladeens in dark cinemas watching Masters of the Universe and me the proud doting Mamma.

The machine I work on has a memory. High Tech they call it. You press buttons and out comes data. You can, press another and wipe it out. Wish I could do that. God, there are some facts in my memory I could do without.

Picture this top dog of a person, like for instance the bishop at confirmation.

'Okay Ms Secretary, produce your memory. Remember the bogs of Ireland you learnt years ago. Remember the seven deadly sins.'

'Pride, covetousness, lust, anger, glutton, envy and sloth, your Grace.'.

'Very good, Ms Secretary, now go back to your seat.'

Sloth sounds sort of nice. I think of an amply-endowed woman on a sofa stuffing herself with chocolates and dangling green grapes from her index finger. And who'd blame her?

I feel slothful now but it wasn't always thus.

There were dancing days when I lined up and got asked out. Was I good-looking? I don't know. Maybe I put men at their ease. I never refused a fella too drunk to stand or a four foot nothing person who'd clutch me round the waist and make me feel like some enormous amazon of a woman. There was one fellow who said, 'Do you ever try your hand at the old courtin'?' That one made me laugh. Should have told him I use the two of them.

I had my share of gentleman callers but nobody stayed for the whole party.

All this and a mother who loved you. Silent and gone from you now to a dreary nursing home. Would be nice if you could bring back the good memories from the past and totally wipe out the present.

Press Delete key, Ms Secretary. Out with the old, in with the new.

So where to now? Not too many choices any more, are there? Set the alarm for tomorrow, out on the floor and off we go with a geranium in your hair.

Dead easy when you don't have to think, isn't it?

# LETTERS FROM LAURETTE

Dear Ex-Husband,

I refer to my note of the 19<sup>th</sup> instant wonder that you have not replied. Has common courtesy gone out the window with you now that you have a new lady friend? What do you think you're at? Do you think by ignoring my correspondence I'll disintegrate?

I realise you are a busy man. What with your dabbling's in the stock exchange, your horse racing, and by no means least or last your entertaining of that bitch of a mistress you have recently acquired. (Never thought I'd descend to that language, but then there are a lot of things I never thought.)

I saw your picture last week in the *Sunday Times*. You were hobnobbing with some sheik or other and Miss Painted Trollop on your arm. I'll give you sheik. There's no doubt about it, life is funny. When I think of darling papa, how right he was about you.

'His people,' he said, 'Mere butchers, love. Don't rush in, darling.' Butchers in every sense of the word. You butchered my heart and made mincemeat of my insides.

Anyway, to the point. As I said, I saw your picture in the paper. That's me - always did read the quality papers. They must be pretty hard up for pictures when they have you and your lady love plastered all over it. (I use the word 'lady' advisedly). I'd like to deliver one large kick to both of you, not to mention your friend the sheikh.

The point of my letter, in any case, dear ex-husband, is that I need some dosh. I'm running out and now need to buy some things - a few winter woollies and suchlike. Also, the house. Oh yes the house. The gutters for one thing. They need gutting, or whatever it is gutters get.

I'm expected to do a man's *and* a woman's job now. So will you please get your act together and by return forward a bankers order in the sum of €10,000. Get  to it and stop your shilly-shallying or you'll be hearing from my solicitors.

Your ex-wife,

Laurette.

P.S.. I don't suppose it bothers you, but do you realise how you've marked our daughter for life.  The poor girl is a nervous wreck.  I know she'll never form a relationship with a good quality decent man because of the role model she's grown up with.  Her latest boyfriend is a plumber from Darndale.  A plumber! Darndale! My beautiful daughter!  I hope you can live with that, darling ex ex ex ex husband.


Dear Angelina,

How are you keeping? I had coffee in the Shelbourne last evening with a yobbo I

picked up in Sachs and you came to mind. We were recalling old times and all the

fun we had.

How do you like life in Zambia? Still wallowing in the heat, I suppose, with little black chappies serving you up vodka and lime day in and day out. Ah me. Such is life. You always knew how to pick them, of course. That was the difference between us. I went for romance and look where that got me

Life in Dublin goes on. I had a vague notion of looking for some sort of work, would you believe, but it's all high tech stuff nowadays. Definitely not my style. . The days of doing a little letter and perhaps filing your nails and having a go at the Simplex in the *Irish Times* seem a time of the past.  Instead I dropped a line to You Know Who. Saw his old puss lately in the paper with some sheikh and his latest squeeze. (That's You Know Who's squeeze, not the sheikh's). What a horse face she is. No doubt had about five facelifts. Her ankles were practically on her forehead. As God made them he matched them. Takes one to know one and all that. Anyway, wrote a letter asking him for a few bob so shall wait and see.

I saw Dolores McConkey in town the other day as well. She looks terrible. She was never exactly a raving beauty but you should see her now. What a decline. I told her she looked great but, my God, has she aged. She's still married to Charlie Berger. They now have, wait for it, eight little sprogs. Once again the mind may be excused for boggling, or whatever it is minds do these days.

Oh, just want to run this by you. Would you consider a trip to the Winter Sports in Switzerland? Talk nicely to that hubby of yours and maybe he'll cough up the necessary. Remember the last time? I mean my ski instructor. Ou la-la. Lord, when I think of it. Not to be repeated, nudge nudge wink wink.

Anyway, I could do with a bit of a lift and maybe you could too. A ski-lift? (No pun intended). There must be some nice men out there but the type you meet these days, my dear Angelina, are, I'm sure you will agree, as common as dirt. It breaks my heart to think about Papa – always immaculate and a proper gent. His heart would bleed for all of us.

Well, give hubby a kiss for me. And perhaps a little cuddle to the black labourer. No offence but I always prefer the golden ones. I suppose you're up to all kinds of tricks while the cat's away. Ha ha, only joking.

Regards and write soon,

Laurette.

P.S. You looked absolutely spiffing in that picture you sent. And what a tan. Really suits you. How do you keep so young looking?. Must be the good life. Or the black servants. (Don't answer that).

Darling Mummy,

Greetings for your birthday. Card and gift to follow. Perhaps one of the kind nursing home staff would read this to you.

I hope all goes well with you and that they're looking after you. I must visit Dunnes and get that woollen vest for you one of these days.

I'm all right myself but a little depressed. Still smarting from the blow of the break-up with Darling Hubbie. He had some nerve but then papa always said he was scum, didn't he? Why do we never listen to our fathers?

I hope the food is good and that they're treating you well in there. They should be for the money they're getting. Daylight robbery if you ask me, but what can one do? It's like getting into heaven in these places now. You'd imagine they were doing you the favour.

I'll call one of these days, mummy but am a little tied up at the minute. I'm sure you understand. Chop chop.

Happy birthday and take care.

Lovingly,

Laurette

Dear Kevin,

Met Dolores McConkey in town recently. She was telling me you and Sybil broke up. Really sorry to hear that, Kev. Listen, I'm in the same boat myself now.

I know you'll find this hard to credit  but Butcher Boy left me high and dry and you should see for what. Face like the back of a bus and roughly twice as large.

Anyhoo... Kevin, this is just to let you know I know the pain and hurt of marriage break-ups at first hand.

I was wondering if you'd feel like an old jar one of these days? The Westbury is *the* place now as you know.  I'm still in Kilmacud and in the book.

Gimme a shout if you feel like it. We could shoot the breeze.

Bestest wishes,

Laurette.

P.S.. I do aerobics twice a week. It's the bee's knees. I've kept my figure more or less. Poor Dolores, she really has let herself go, don't you think?

Dear Beth,

I hope you're well and studying hard. You do need that degree, sweetheart. Money doesn't grow on trees, you know. I meant to call over to the north side for a visit last weekend but as you know I dread crossing the Liffey. I hope by now you've broken off with that plumber chap.

Don't get me wrong, I could never be called a snob, but Beth darling, a *plumber*. It would never work. So, give that fellow the chop as soon as you can.

On second thought, maybe not. I just had a thought. I wonder does he do gutter work? Maybe you could put a word in his ear about a little job for your mummy. *Then* break if off. Is that very mean of your mummy?????

And now to me.

What with visiting gran in the nursing home and the heartbreak of your father leaving me etc. I feel I need it's now 'Be nice to Laurette' time.

This year it would be a good idea if you spent Xmas with your father, darling. I have some plans for myself, you see. Nothing cast in stone but vaguely thinking of taking a trip to the sun this year.

What would you think? Anything to get out of this dump. Xmas is such a lonely time for a separated lady, isn't it?

Take care,

Fondly,

Mummy

Dear Dolores,

I've been thinking of you all week since we bumped into each other.

How do you keep looking so young, Dolores? Especially with all those kids. No doubt you and Charlie are absolute marvels.

You mentioned you were having a little get-together for Christmas. I just happen to be free that night.

As I told you, I was left rather suddenly by my 'life' partner (ha ha) and I wouldn't wish to interfere with Beth's Christmas, especially with mother being in the nursing home.

Oh dear, when I think of papa - it would have devastated him.

Anyway, I'd just love to see you and Charlie, and of course the eight little ones. We could have an old-fashioned Dickensian Christmas. What say you?

Is Meath a bit far away, by the way? Perhaps I could drive down on Christmas Eve and stay until the New Year.

Interesting about Kevin Sheehan.

You know what, Dolores – wouldn't it be an idea to invite him along? It's nice to be nice, isn't it?

Expecting to hear from you.

Soonish,

Love and best wishes to Charlie and the kiddies.

Laurette.

P.S. I was going through my mail and looking at a picture of Angelina. A recent one. You know she's out in Zambia with that idiot of a husband of hers, don't you?

Gosh, Dolores, we could be her daughters. She looks just like a shrivelled prune. Must be the sun.   Again, lots of love to Charlie.

Dear Jasmine,

I don't normally read the lighter Sunday papers but I was very impressed with the article last week in one of them (can't remember which) about your appearance on the *Late Late,* which I sadly missed seeing.

I understand you've written some articles on how to find love in this crazy world.

I'm a young woman – around the forty mark – and have been, as they say, dumped by a dirty scheming rat of a husband.

However, I'm not one to bear a grudge.

I shall get to the point. I'm a very sexual and attractive woman, Jasmine, but I find it really impossible to meet a desirable man in this town.

I just learned recently of an old flame becoming, as they say, 'available' again.

He's a very successful businessman, not that that means anything to me. (I was never impressed by wealth, as you know. Always go for the *inner* man).

Anyhow, I believe he's been separated from his wife for some time.

I thought perhaps you could offer advice on how I might organise a get-together.

I've contacted a mutual acquaintance with this in mind but for some unfathomable reason she still hasn't got back to me. As someone said, it's not just dog-eat-dog in this godforsaken world of ours anymore,it's dog won't return dog's phone calls.  And that drives me bonkers. Would it not you? Patience was never my virtue, as you know.

I also dropped the man himself a note, totally innocent, I might add. This also drew a blank. So where do I turn now? Frustrating, oh so frustrating.

With very best wishes,

Laurette.

P.S. I keep myself well and could pass for the late twenties any day of the week if the light is favourable.

# THE STONE AGE GIRL

In appearance she was as you would expect. Your typical secretarial type of specimen of the female form. No distinguishing features, no birthmarks, nothing to separate her from the common run.

In stature she was tall, measuring 5ft 7ins in her stocking vamps. Her father had introduced her to the term 'vamps'. She didn't know the exact meaning of the word. However, being of average intelligence, she concluded it to refer to being minus a pair of shoes.

Her figure was neither slender nor, as they say nowadays, morbidly obese. Her hair colour was a mousy brown. In the summer time some streaks of blonde showed themselves but this was only when there were lengthy periods of sunshine. Her skin changed to a warm brown shade during those summer days. When the weather cooled down her colouring returned to its customary milky whiteness.

Her father was a spiritual person. He attended to his religious duties, , religiously. He confessed his sins every second Saturday and never missed Mass on Sundays or Holy Days of Obligation He fasted fastidiously during the forty days of Lent and was generous to the poor, making donations to the upkeep of the parish, the St Vincent de Paul, the little black children in Africa and the St Joseph's Young Priests Society.

He worked all his life as a sorter in the Post Office, breathing his last breath while placing the letters for Dublin 3 in the appropriate delivery bag. The cause of death was a clot to the brain. His funeral was attended by many neighbours and workmates. They sang his praises and talked about his honesty, his integrity and his high place in heaven. She grieved for her father and forever after wore his gold medal for Senior Hurling on a chain around her neck.

Her mother, Angela, had different kinds of ambitions for herself, which she never achieved, and ambitions for her daughter. She too was religious and observed all the rules, standing side by side with her husband at all novenas, missions and even once on a trip to Lourdes.

Angela performed well during her schooldays, getting four honours in the Intermediate Certificate. The honours were in Mathematics, Geography, History and Religious Knowledge, but because of a lack of money she was forced to leave school before she did her Leaving Certificate.

This was a cause of great disappointment to her. She had a strong belief that if the opportunity was open to her daughter she would now be a qualified teacher instead of spending three years serving up meals in the Regional Hospital.

Angela met her husband when she was seventeen at a dance in Seapoint Ballroom. The Dixies were playing that night and she'd fallen in love on the spot. They were upstairs in the balcony when Cupid's arrow went to her heart. The rest, as they say, is history.

Though satisfied in her love life and her marriage, Angela still carried resentment that she hadn't become a teacher, or perhaps a doctor, or even a low grade civil servant, destined to rise through the years to become a Higher Executive Officer, as was the case with the Flaherty one from Fair Hill.

She pinned such hopes on her daughter but, sad to tell, they weren't realised by her either. In fact she barely squeezed through the Inter Cert. This caused her enormous guilt. She didn't go on to do the Leaving, instead enrolling in a secretarial course in the local Technical College. The shame of being there caused her mother to lose sleep many nights. She hid the fact as best she could when chatting to other mothers whose daughters were planning to go to UCG and achieve Great Things.

The Girl struggled with the basics of the secretarial course. She never mastered shorthand and was delighted when it became obsolete. She did manage to learn to touch-type, only now and again taking a squint at the top row on the typewriter where all the numbers were. After a year she worked briefly in a hospital, doing relief work in the accounts department.  She eventually got a position in an office selling life insurance. It was located in Dublin Four in the heart of the business belt.  Here she became, like her colleagues, a fully-fledged Performing Seal.

She got a flat in Clontarf and stayed in the job for many years, in time becoming promoted from junior typist to secretary to the Top Man in the job, even being allowed to check his appointments for him in time, and make tea for himself and foreign dignitaries when they called to visit him for Important Meetings.

The Girl rose on weekday mornings at 8 minutes past 7 without the use of an alarm clock. She washed her hair and dressed and then got herself ready for the 8.25 Dart to her place of employment, sitting with her hands folded neatly all the way in with a pleased expression on her face.

After she got to her office she said a friendly good morning to all the other typists, even the junior ones, and then plugged in her ear gadgets and typed away all the Important Letters the Top Man gave her to type until 25 minutes past five, at which point she folded her files, straighten her skirt and put on her coat.

She did this every year from Monday to Friday each week except for her two weeks in the summer when she usually went to Bundoran, and a week at Christmas that she spent with her mother.

Lest you imagine her life was boring, she did have a lover, though she wasn't his first choice. He had been married years ago but it was broken up now. When he saw The Girl it was love at first sight. They saw each other once a week for the first few months and then more and more. After three years of romance they moved in together, getting themselves a small arty dwelling house off the Howth Road.

The Girl's lover was a housepainter.  Each room in their little abode was lovingly painted in delicious pastel shades, his attention to detail being second to none.  She sometimes thought he was wasted, that he could have been a famous interior designer if he put his mind to it. He was kind and caring as well and listened to her talking about all her stresses in the workplace.

As time passed and modern technology took over, her confidence deserted her more and more. He gave her support and love but the hours in the office were long and the Girl began to feel she'd lost her skills, if indeed she ever had them. Finally the Top Man retired and was replaced by a Young Ambitions man. Then fear set in.

To be fair to her, she gave it her all. She managed to master the language of computers and to learn off by heart the relevant procedures that were required.

'Cop on to yourself,' the housepainter told her, 'At the end of the day it's all typing, just fancier language.'

'Look Missus,' she'd say to herself, 'You had it easy for years. Every day was normal and average. Now you're out of your routine. You have to learn about mice and Windows and God knows what else they throw at you, even rats.'

But it was no good. No matter how many pep talks she gave herself she was still a ball of nerves.

Sometimes she thought she hadn't grown up at all. She had nightmares about how bad she was in school in the 'Pres' in Galway. She'd go back in her mind to horrible things like sums, or graphs, or geometry. The Girl never understood graphs. She drew them without knowing what she saw drawing. When they were finished she saw them as little hills. She thought they should be a part of the Art class, not the Maths one. She knew she'd have had great fun working on them there. Sometimes she put climbers on them, and flags at the top. This caused the teachers to go crazy. 'Child!' they'd roar, 'You have to use coordinates, not climbers!' But she never knew what things like coordinates were.

After a few years The Girl stopped going to Bundoran. Instead she spent her summer holidays with her mother. She also stayed with her over the Christmas. Her mother was now crippled with arthritis and seriously depressed. Sometimes she would tell The Stone Age Girl what a disappointment she'd been to her, and she an only daughter. The Stone Age Girl would think of her mother's clever brain and it would almost break her heart that she was such a disappointment to her. She understood her mother's sadness, realising she had hopes of a husband of high calibre for her only child.

One Stephen's Day when they sat in the dark together, not even plugging in the Christmas tree  lights, her mother told her she'd bought a dress and jacket in Anthony Ryan's - mauve and very classy – that she planned to wear on The Stone Age Girl's wedding day.

As the housepainter was a separated man, God between us and all harm, the Girl never said much about him to her mother, just vaguely mentioning that he wasn't the marrying kind, nor she either. She said she was more interested in 'going places' in the insurance office. She felt this would keep her mother happy.  She told her she had now mastered computers and was in line for a Serious Promotion one of these days. She said this so much that eventually she came to believe it.

But one day in June 2004, everything in the office came to a head. She was sitting at her screen typing away like billyo, moving the mouse about and feeling reasonably secure in herself when suddenly her mind went blank.

Suddenly she couldn't remember a single thing she'd learnt.

All the times of not knowing came together in her mind.

She saw younger brighter girls working away to beat the band, girls like the Healy sisters.

Then the room started to spin.

 When she looked down at the mouse on her computer she saw that it had grown ears and a long curly tail.

Next of all the creature started to speak.

'Will you look at yourself,' it squeaked, 'You're past your sell-by date. You're useless, feckin' bloody useless.'

The letters jumbled up on the screen and her face got hot. She rose from her seat and left the room. Into the Ladies with her and she sat on the floor crying.

'God help me,' she said, 'what will I do? I'm bunched, I'm no good.'

After a time one of the brighter younger girls, Samantha, knocked at the door. A bit of a consequence she was.

'Are you all right, in there,' she called, 'Any probs?'

She came out from the toilet. She knew her eyes were red but she didn't care. Back into the typing room she went where all the young and more clever Performing Seals sat.

Taking up her position she pulled out her drawers from her desk.

Old pictures from ten years ago looked out at her. So did a letter from a penfriend, a few lipsticks and a packet of soggy cigarettes. Symbols of her fulfilled career.

She took the drawer and flung it on the ground with a vengeance. Then she threw the mouse down beside it.

'Excuse me,' said the lady supervisor, 'Are you okay? What are you doing?'

The Girl now felt quite pleased with herself. She rose from her desk and went over and got her coat from the rack where she always left it at 8.55 every morning.

'I'm going,' she said. 'I'm off.'

'Off? Off where?' said the supervisor.

'Anywhere,' she replied. 'Maybe Russia. Maybe outer space.'

'Now you're being ridiculous,' said the supervisor, 'Come back this instant and sit down. And put the mouse back on your desk.'

'You can keep your old mouses,' said The Girl. 'Keep your mouses and send me out my P45. Or better still, stick it where the monkey sticks the nuts. I'm resigning.'

'Sit down, sit down,' said the supervisor lady, 'You're obviously not well. Can we phone for a doctor for you? Or maybe your husband, oh sorry, partner? I can see you're upset. Perhaps you need a rest for a few days.'

'No,' said The Girl, 'Maybe *you* need a rest.'

She heard a few of the young ones giggling at all this. One of them was whispering about The Change of Life.

'It affects people in different ways,' said Samantha.

'She didn't even know how to Skype,' the fat red-haired one put in.

'Or to tweet' said another one.

'Or to use Facebook,' said a third. A fourth said she wasn't even sure The Girl had a mobile.

'She must be from the Stone Age,' said a fifth.

And so it came to pass that from there on she was known as The Stone Age Girl.

Next off, Mr O'Brien from Accounts arrived in. He had obviously heard everything that was going on.

'Take it easy, my dear,' he said, 'You need a break. I'll drive you home. Don't worry. You'll be fine in a few days.'

She pushed him aside shouting, 'I'm all right, let me go.'

But he wasn't to be deterred. He grabbed her arm and pulled her out of the office. Before she knew what was happening she was out in the car park.

'What are you doing?' she said, disentangling herself from him.

'I'm bringing you home,' he said, 'That's what.'

A minute later she was in his car.

At the office window more goggling staff stood gaping..

'This was a long time coming,' said Samantha, 'I knew there was something funny about that one the first time I clapped eyes on her.'

All the way home she kept imagining the talk of them. As well as The Stone Age Girl, they were now referring to her as Miss Confused Dot.Com.

Mr O'Brien didn't speak to her, he just looked kindly at her when they were stopped at the lights. He was also, she thought, a little bit frightened of her. Maybe he thought she'd make a dash for freedom.

When they got to her house he looked at her as if he was getting himself ready for a big chat.

'Can I come in?' he asked, 'Is Peter home? You need a doctor, girl. It's stress. It hits the best of us by times.'

She rushed out of the car and banged the door. A disappointed Mr O'Brien drove off

When she got inside her house she saw Pete wasn't at home. She made herself a cup of tea and threw herself onto the sofa. It was one they'd got in Arnotts made of lovely soft leather. She could still hear the horrible laughing of mouse and the girls as she sat down and tried to calm herself.

When Peter came home she was sleeping.

'Wake up,' he said, 'Wake up, my love. What are you doing home at this hour of the day? Are you sick?'

'No,' she said, 'I'm not sick, I've taken early retirement, Pete. I can't take any more of that place. I walked out.'

'Surely not! You can't have done that. You're far too young for retirement.'

'I can and I have,' she said, 'and I'm not.'

'But what will you do? How will you fill the days?'

'Maybe I'll train mice,' she said.

'Now you're raving, my dear,' he told her, 'I'll make you a cup of tea.'

She drank tea as if it was going out of fashion for the rest of the day. Then she sat down with a nice novel she'd been putting off reading for years. It was about a rabbit who lived in a shoe. All the while Peter looked oddly at her as if he was expecting her to leap out of the seat or something.

She slept soundly that night but Peter didn't. He sat by her bedside as if he expected her to wake up raving at any moment.

A few days later a deputation from the office arrived out to the house.

'How are you?' said Samantha, the head bottle-washer, 'We brought flowers.'

She handed her a lovely bunch of carnations.

'You shouldn't have bothered,' she told her.

'It was no bother. Now you just get yourself well. Don't come back tilll you're good and ready. Mrs Anderson says they might send you on a refresher course when you come back. Everything will be fine.'

'Yes,' she said, 'everything will be fine.'

God love them, she thought, they'd only escaped briefly from their little zoo..

That weekend Pete had to go out of town.

'Will you be okay?' he said, 'I don't like leaving you.'

'Don't worry,' she said, 'I promise not to burn the house down, or even attack any mice.'

On the following Saturday morning she decided she was going to fulfil a lifetime plan. After washing her hair and having a shower she went to the Dart station the same as she always did at 8.25. She travelled to town looking every inch the pert secretary with her hands neatly folded over her lap.

When she got to the office she let herself in with a key she'd kept for herself without the top brass knowing.

As she got to her desk she hung her coat up on the rack. She allowed herself a little glance at the clock. It pleased her that it didn't say 8.55.

Everything was still and silent in the office. Empty seats sat facing empty silent screens and scores of mice huddled up on desks waiting for the Performing Seals to return on Monday.

The first thing she did was lock all the windows so birdies couldn't send in any tweets. She also locked the other kind of windows, Word for Windows.

She waited for a minute and then wiped her hands in glee before pulling the mice from their sockets. Then she flung them in a mass of tangles into the centre of the floor. Afterwards she threw chunks of cheese at them, and large dollops of mouse poison.

'Eat up, my boyos,' she said, 'Enjoy yourselves.'

She turned on screens and saw them flashing and glinting. They all demanded names and passwords so she keyed in some of her own creation. Mickey Mouse. Bugs Bunny. Igor Stravinsky – that kind of thing.

'Are you sure?' asked one computer.

'Yes,' she replied, 'I was never surer of anything in my life.'

Then she went to the filing cabinets behind where Mrs Anderson sat. She pulled out all the files she could find, put them into a bundle and set a match to them.

Others she simply tore them to shreds. (It was getting to be quite fun now). She threw the mashed-up balls of paper at the mice.

'Eat up,' she said again, 'Eat up, my little friends, you must be ravenous sitting there all day without any Seals to feed you.'

As she was leaving the building, Mr O'Brien pulled up in his car.

'Hello, there,' he said. 'It's good to see you. How are you feeling?'

'Fine,' she said.

'Come back with me and have a cup of tea,' he offered, 'You look a bit flushed.'

'No thanks,' she said.

'But you look poorly,' Mr Anderson persisted.

'It's okay,' she said, 'it's just the change of life.'

'The change of life?'

'Yes. I don't love Seals or Mouses anymore. I've changed.'

Mr Anderson looked perplexed as she giggled and walked off.

A few weeks later The Stone Age Girl got herself a job with different kinds of seals, the ones that live in oceans. She joined a Save the Seal group and went all around the world trying to preserve the species.

One day she met the other kind of Seals, the Performing Ones, in Bewley's for a coffee. They told her they heard what she did that day in the office, or at least what she was suspected of doing. Her action had resulted in an increased respect for them all. They'd got an increase of 4%, even though Mr O'Brien had to call in experts from America to repair all the computers. They spent seven weeks working day and night and now all the mouses are fine again and squeaking away to their heart's content.

Her mother lived to the ripe old age of 98. During her final years her mind became muddled and once in the spring of 2013 Pete and The Stone Age Girl brought her on a bus tour to Ballybunion. One evening towards the end of the tour the three of them joined the other tourists to the bar for a sing-song, Angela was wearing the mauve dress and jacket from Anthony Ryan's. She was telling a large man from Liverpool that she was accompanied by her darling daughter and her very loving husband.

'I couldn't ask for a better girl,' she said, 'even if she *is* from the Stone Age. 'She has brains to burn and has devoted her life to Saving Seals. Her husband, who's a pure gentleman, teaches dolphins how to tap-dance in his spare time. He is a qualified Marine Biologist, so they are well suited.'

The man from Liverpool, who had Irish blood in him, told the old lady it was lovely to see a family so united.

The old lady smiled and replied, 'Family is everything. Her daddy was a man in a million, senior advisor to the Minister for

Posts & Telegraphs. My daughter used to work in an old folk's home but later on went up to set up her own computer business, which she calls Confused Dot.Com. Now she is focussing on marine life round the Irish Coast. Brains to burn, I tell you, brains to burn,'

It was true. The Stone Age Girl now works from home. Since that day in the office she lost all her fears of technology. Confusion, in fact, is her preferred state of mind. She finds if she presses keys without thinking of them everything usually turns out right.

The man from Liverpool was so friendly that the Girl's mother took a crumpled letter from her handbag and gave it to him. She wanted him to admire her daughter's work.

'Dear Yhjlfodovoboodddfftgp' it went, 'How is fgtynhjuiuuuuu. Xyhnhjy. Sincerely Dfkgjcwiuuucuo ocococfffgght.'

The man from Liverpool wasn't quite sure how to respond.

'Um, yes,' he muttered. Whereupon The Stone Age Girl's partner gave him a friendly pat on the back.

Everything is going hunky dory now in the girl's office as she works from home. Her hard drive did get a virus once but she got the Computer Doctor in and he gave it antibiotics. She sat up with it all night and dandled it in her arms with a soother. In the end it turned out to be just a three day bug so it's fine now. She just needs to give it a kiss now and then and tell it she loves it to prevent it feeling lonely or sick. Kisses also keep the hackers away.

To prevent any further mishaps she's installed mousetraps all around it in case any more little rodents start to sprout ears after she clicks the mouse to get online.

She's also removed all the locks on her windows so now birds can tweet as much as they bloody well like.

As long as they don't put them on Facebook.

# NOTHING TO LOSE

It's funny the people you hear from. I hadn't the foggiest who he was when I picked up the phone. Was it a crank call? Was he one of those weirdos you hear about you get your number somehow and then try to get off with you?

'Don't tell me you forget the Singles Dance in '87' he said.

'I well could have,' I told him.

'It was definitely '87,' he said, 'because I broke up with the wife the year before. I seem to remember you had a penfriend in Finland at the time.'

'That's right. I went over to see him afterwards.'

'And?'

'Well it didn't work out.'

'These things never really do, do they? I mean a romance conducted by post can't be the real deal, can it?'

I supposed not, and it was then he suggested we meet for a quick one to shoot the breeze. No strings, of course. He just wanted the old trip down Memory Lane.

Memory Lane? I hardly knew him from Adam. But I must have given him my phone number. Maybe I was getting senile. Loss of memory one of the first signs. I told him I'd see him in the Shelbourne Hotel. What had I to lose?

I recognized him the minute I got to the hotel. Tall and fair and a kind of open look about him. You'd definitely know he was a farmer. That's it – the farmer with marriage troubles from West Cork - as distinct from the one from the midlands who lost his wife in an accident, or the one from Galway who never married and joined the Knock Bureau once. Just the once mind you. But no luck there. Met a nurse from outside Kells, he told me, but too much mileage on the old clock for his liking. That famous clock. My own one was tick-tocking away fast too, but maybe this was it. Maybe the farmer from West Cork and myself would make a go of it.

He was generous anyway, I had to give him that. Took me to dinner he did and was quite good-humoured also. He was a snappy dresser too – nice beige trousers round his short legeens. The height obviously came from his upper bod. He was smelling sweetly of Expensive Men's Stuff. So clearly making an effort..

We had a few jars and chilled out, as the Yanks say. He was drinking pints and me half-pints.

'Are you still with the accountants in Merrion Square?' he asked.

'Yes, still there I'm afraid. You have to stay put nowadays with the economy the way it is, don't you? No hope of another job if I left.'

'That's true, things are bad all over.'

'Now you said it.'

And so we rattled and prattled on and on. I went to the Ladies once and was pleased to see my face hadn't gone the bright red it sometimes goes from drink. Then back again to Snappy Dresser. Into the breach rode the 600, or whatever they say.

He seemed glad to see me return. Things were looking up.

'You'll have another, won't you?' he asked, 'or maybe a small one this time. Most women don't go for the beer.'

'No, the beer is fine, thanks.'

In West Cork in green wellington Mrs Farmerette is seen splashing the white milk from the udders of the cow into a shiny silver bucket. Or is she? Maybe with modern technology the whole job is now done in milking parlours with machines blaring away while the poor cow dreams of the dairy maids who used to gently squeeze the milk from him, meanwhile signing ditties about blue-eyed boys who were now in America.

In the meantime, cherry-cheeked children sit on top of haystacks and little chickens chirp round a sunny garden while Farmer Joe whistles away as the days nears its close. No more Account Balance Sheets or word processor menus. No, now the menu would be apple pie baked by Mrs ICA, who just happens to be this year's Housewife Of The Year to boot.

'I really wanted to see you because I value your opinion,' he said, which caused me to splutter. I almost sprayed him with a mouthful of beer which was busily going down the wrong way.

'My opinion?'.

'Yes. You see I'm in the same boat you were in all those years ago with the fellow from Finland. Do you get my drift? Pardon the pun. You know – Boat? Drift?' He poked me in the ribs quite hard. It was a bit obscure but I managed to give a little laugh.

'She's actually from Austria. I met her last summer at the Rose of Tralee. She was a bit worried about the culture gap but she's a fine-looking woman. She loves Ireland too.'

'Is she in Ireland now?'

'Yes. She's doing a computer course in Cork. Actually she's joining us later. You're not in a mad rush, are you?'

This put a different complexion on things. What was I – an old flame or an agony aunt? Goodbye Mrs Farmerette.

'Well actually I have to meet a friend later on. You said just a quick drink, didn't you?' What did he think I was – a professional gooseberry?

'Right, fine. That's a pity, though. I always felt you were a sound sort of woman. I knew you'd be a good judge of character.'

'Thank you,' I said, trying to be as withering as possible. 'Well I suppose that's it then.'

I was sobering up at the rate of knots.

I stood up. Always hated time-wasters.

Obviously he didn't see it that way.

'Listen, it was great to see you again, Give us a shout if you're down in West Cork anytime. With a bit of luck myself and Helga will be together in the near future and we can hook up. Maybe you could bring your Finnish friend as well. Being foreigners they might have something in common.'

I was still in shock but I'm a good actress in situations like that. I put on my best poker face.

'Sure. that's right, Anyway, all the best. And thanks for the drinks.'

'On the contrary, thank *you*. It was a real blast to see you.'

A blast? I thought only Yanks said that. Maybe he was doing me a favour going off with Helga. I thought I could happily live the rest of my life not being tied to a man who used expressions like 'a blast.'

I got out of there as fast as my legs could carry me. Outside the weather was vicious. I didn't feel like freezing to death at a bus stop so I decided to hail a passing taxi. I needed a little treat to stop my anger.

My opinion indeed. He wasn't that great anyway. A bit of a drip really. Welcome to his old Helga so he was. I hoped it kept fine for them. Could just see them out for some grub in Kinsale at some nifty little fish place. Quite a snob in his own way really. Culchies usually the worst ones I always thought.

I sat into the taxi. The driver smiled at me through his rear view mirror. I hated smiley taxi drivers. They always thought they knew more than you did. All I needed now was for him to start talking about politics. Or soccer.

'Going home early, love?' he said, 'Have a row with the boyfriend?'

It was none of his bloody business but I decided to answer him anyway.

'No, not really. I was just meeting an old acquaintance for a drink.'

'Oh, an old acquaintance. Not a boyfriend then?'

'Excuse me?'

I always said that when I wanted to be snotty to someone.

'I'm sorry,' he said, 'I'm being nosey.'

At least he had the decency to apologise.

'It's all right. No, he wasn't a boyfriend.'

'You know what?' he said then, 'You're a very nice-looking girl.'

Compliments were so rare these days his words made me feel good. I smiled at him and he smiled back. This time it didn't seem so bad.

He fastened his eyes on me like lasers.

'You wouldn't fancy joining me for a scoop some evening, would you, love? I mean that about you being nice-looking. I'm not just saying it.'

Was he for real? Planning a date after knowing me five seconds?

I was on the horns of a dilemma. First The Farmer and now Mr Taxi-Man. Would I be going from the frying pan into the fire?

He was no oil painting. Red face and a mean little mouth. Never trust a man with a small mouth, they said. Still, you never knew. Love can happen at any time. Take your chances while they came, Mammy always said.

'I don't know,' I said, but as I was paying him he pressed me more and I ended up putting my phone number on a piece of paper.

'I'm not saying I will, now,' I told him, 'I'm just saying I might.'

'That'll do me,' he said, 'You've made my day.' '

He waved the money away and told me to put it in my pocket. A nice gesture.

Or was he on a promise? Some men were like that. Felt they owned you if they did some tiny little thing like that.

I walked up the street wondering if I'd let myself in for something I mightn't be able to get out of – again.

Should really have written the wrong number. That was one of my usual tricks in the old days. Maybe I had more offers then.

Inside the house I had another beer and then got my hot water bottle. You can't beat the old bed on a cold night, can you? In many ways it's better than a man. At least you didn't have to entertain a hot water bottle. And it didn't walk out on you the next morning.

I found it hard to sleep, probably as a result of all the beer. Yer man was also bothering me. What a cheek leading me on like that and then dropping that bomb on me.

What an ego. Could have understood it if he had something to boast about but he didn't. And that tie! Holy God, talk about shocking pink. Probably meant to impress Helga.

Could just picture the little bitch in Austria, pulling the poor cow's udders with her big strong hands. Yodelling away to beat the band.

Yo ho, happy days making milk for sweetie.

Put them all out of your mind, I told myself. Try to get some shuteye. Maybe next week I'd give that Singles place another go.

Or your man the taxi fellow might ring.

He wasn't that bad really. Honest looking. Sort of gentle. You could do worse, as they said. Definitely not married.

That was a big plus, though you could never tell these days. Could have taken off the gold band. The Romeos all did that.

I wondered if we could have made a go of it.

Never saw myself as a taxi-man's wife. I'd worry about him out at night probably if we were married. So many crazies out there now, pulling knives on you to save a few punts.

City not safe for man or beast. And the little lady at home with the heart crossways in her worrying about the fact that the man in her life was possibly lying in a gutter somewhere.

The bottle got cold so I filled it again.

When I was down in the kitchen I got myself two fig rolls as well. You had to be nice to yourself, didn't you? No one else was.

Yes, the taxi driver.

He definitely looked promising.

Could well be the one for me.

Stranger things have happened.

I'll give him a chance anyway.

It would be nice not to have to pay the fare for a change.

# I WAS THERE

Dear Donald,

Hold onto that hat of yours. Make yourself a cup of strong tea and then get youself a comfy seat because I have something major to tell you. Plenty of sugar, Donald. It's good for shock. Deep breaths please. In and out, out and in.

We've seen all the Laurel & Hardy movies, right? We've read the books. But who can stand up and tell people they planted their feet on the very soil, the very soil, Donald, when Stan lived before he was, dare I say, Stan Laurel?

I did that, Donald. Maybe one day you can too.

They say he was Clint Eastwood's father. They say he was the supporting player in the L&H series. But we know different, don't we, Donald?

As long as I live, my friend, I doubt I shall ever recover from the experience of the past few months. I may not have pressed Stan's flesh, I may not have inhabited the time he inhabited, I may not have eaten the bread he ate or drank the drinks he drank, but by God I tried. I went as close as dammit to all that.

I was there, Donald. I was in the place he breathed, the place he grew up, the place he formed his first thoughts, the place he took his first steps. And my heart is still beating from the excitement. It was just two days ago, to be precise.

Ulverston. How many people have heard about it? How many people want to? God have pity on them.

At 4 p.m. on Friday 7th June I stood at Stan Laurel's birthplace. Remember that fact, Donald. Remember it as long as you live.

Dum di dum. Dum di dum, Dum diddy dum diddy dum dum dum.

Of course you know where it is, don't you? You know everything about him, even more than me, perhaps.

Isn't it nice to share a twin obsession about an unadulterated genius?

It's a small place, Ulverston. Nothing much to look at. You could pass by it without ever knowing you were there.

Heard a man say he went there once but it was closed. Ho ho.

Maybe people could say the same about Jerusalem or the Holy Land, couldn't they? Ah but you can get too touristy. Sometimes, as we both know, sometimes the most ordinary place can produce the most extraordinary person in this mysterious world of ours.

'The visit,' as I call it, will stay forever in my mind. I was wearing my special tie and had my hair combed just right. Such details are important. One has to create the mood, doesn't one?

In fact my ensemble was even better than the night when you and I did the show for the Old Folks last Christmas.

But enough of that. Now it's time for… 'The Visit'. I shall spare you the boring details of the rest of my trip and lead up gradually to The Moment so you too can savour it.

The trip over was uneventful. Maybe Christopher Columbus' first trip to America was also uneventful, before he knew it was there, if you know what I mean.

I wasn't seasick, though felt a little bit queasy. I brought ten of my videos with me but unfortunately they didn't have a video machine on the ferry. However, there was one in the little B & B I stayed in which actually turned out to be quite pleasant.

It was a small stone house just outside a place called something like Windermere-on-Bowness in the heart of the Lake District. (Don't those English-y places all sound the same, showing off their bloody rivers?)

The landlady was an old dear, though. And, wonders of wonders, she was a fan. Talk about the luck of the Irish. In the evenings we both watched my videos from 7 until bedtime, which was bloody marvellous. Sorry about all the 'bloody, pardon my French'.

I decided I'd keep the best wine until last and as Mrs Higglethwaite (the landlady) had a small motor car, we toured about every day. To be honest, I think she fancied me but she was definitely not my type.

We called to Wordsworth's home *en route* but it was a pale imitation of what was to follow. Also saw Grasmere.

Did you know Willie Wordsworth lived to be a ripe old age? Always pictured him as a sickly youth lying on that couch of his in vacant and pensive food. Apparently the old geezer lived into his eighties, but there you go. You live and learn.

Mrs H. and myself then took a trip into Yorkshire.

Saw a bit of the dales and fells as well. Treated myself to a boat trip too and a jaunt, would you believe, on a steam engine.

My trusty landlady made an excellent travelling companion and I was able to keep her at a distance as regards the old romance. Not very well educated, mind you, but a certain natural peasant instinct which was jolly endearing.

Unfortunately the old dear had a problem with varicose veins so she sat in the car for much of our trips. She spent most of her time reading romantic novels, while yours truly, intrepid as ever, wandered lonely as a cloud and took in all the local beauty spots.

I found I developed quite an appetite as a result and treated Mrs H. to dinner on two occasions. Menu quite good and not too pricey. Mrs H. went for roast beef, but *moi*, fearing Mad Cow Disease, contented myself with good old reliable chicken. Also took the odd glass of *vino*. (And why not, sez you).

On the evening of the visit I was very strung up. As luck would have it, Mrs H. suffers from her nerves so she gave me a mild tranquilliser the night before. This helped a little.

We left home early the next day. The weather was cloudy but the rain, T.G., held off. We stopped at a spot called Barrow-in-Furness for a coffee. Not a great place but quaint in its way.

Picked up a few nic-nacs in a tourist shop for the relatives back home, you know those things that cost the earth and are about as big as your fingernail. Mrs H. insisted on paying for the meal because she wanted to return my hospitality for the two meals I mentioned.

I forced myself to have soup, lamb cutlets, two veg, carrots and sprouts, and some French fries.

Had a light dessert of apple crumble to round it all off. This was slightly underdone and lay a bit on my old tum, I'm afraid. I think you're aware of my problem with constipation but I suffered in silence because I didn't want to upset Mrs H., especially after her paying and all. It might have sounded ungracious. Anyway, a minor problem. I soon forget all about it.

It was four p.m. on the dot when we arrived at Ulverston. Four p.m. on Friday, the 7th June. A real red letter day.

The museum is tucked away off the main street, Donald. The town itself is small and nondescript, nothing exceptional, but of course that didn't matter under the circumstances.

We found Stan's house no problem. As well as the museum they have a small cinema which runs Laurel & Hardy films, would you believe, all day.

They showed one of his life too, and then an old gentleman, the curator of the museum, delivered a lecture on his childhood and later career. Fantastic fare altogether.

Wonder of wonders, the old boy's uncle knew him personally? He had such a collection of memorabilia you could spend a year going through it if you were that way inclined.

As I'm Irish he presented me with a picture of Stan's arrival in Cobh. The Mayor of Cork greeted him and the local paper took the picture. What a keepsake. I bet you are positively green with envy.

The curator, as I said, has a wonderful collection. Stan lived with his grandma as a small boy and there was a wonderful collection of old photographs of this time too. Fab stuff indeed. Afterwards the old gent invited us back to his place.

He was thrilled to meet genuine fans like us. Apparently the locals are totally ignorant about it all. What's that about one about people never being prophets in their own land? Whatever.

Anyway, the curator is trying to build an eight foot statue of Stan in the centre of the town. Marvellous idea, what?

I decided it was such a worthy cause I gave him a fiver towards it. Should help towards a few bits of stone. I'm going to keep in touch with the old boy, Donald, because he really has some whopping insights.

Mrs H. and myself wound up the day by having a few drinks in a local hostelry. Mrs H. was hitting the bottle a bit hard so I insisted on driving home. I think the whole experience was too much for the old dear.

I'm enclosing some postcards of Stan and Ollie. The curator also had some info on Ollie but as we all know,

Stan was the real genius of the twosome. By the by, I got a local yokel to take the enclosed snap outside Stan's house. As you can see, Mrs H. is no Helen of Troy but never mind. The curator isn't in the first flush either, which makes my good self (says he with all humility) the beauty of the bunch.

By now you will have gathered that it will take me a long time to recover from this mind-boggling odyssey. I know money is tight for you what with mortgage, the kiddies shoes and whatever, not to mention your lady wife's recent gall bladder op, but someday you might consider making the trip with me.

All you'd need is the cost of your fare. I know Mrs H. would put us up at a reduced rate. If you're strapped for cash I'd be glad to treat you to a meal or two. Think about it, Donald. Maybe, when they unveil Stan's statue.

Anyhow, here's hoping to see you in this neck of the woods in the meantime. I see they're showing a documentary on Channel 4 next Tuesday at midnight: *Laurel and Hardy's Laughing Twenties*. I know you have it on video but sometimes nice to see it live, so to speak.

Well I'll sign off now. Dum di dum. Dum di Dum. Dum diddy dum diddy dum dum dum. I've enjoyed sharing this with you. A real once-in-a-lifetime experience.

As ever,

Your old school pal,

Ambrose

P.S. Hope you don't take offence about my comments on Stan being the brains of the duo. I know you do a brilliant imitation of Ollie but this is just because you're a little larger than me (ha ha). Again, hope no offence but I do keep myself trim and get plenty of exercise.

Also, of course, I have more opportunities to look after myself, not having any responsibilities. And what better person to have to look after than yours truly?

Much love to you and yours from your dear and trusted friend, Donald. May all your troubles be little ones. Ho ho

# NOT A DRESS REHEARSAL

He told her in the September. She knew it was coming when he asked her to sit down and leave the dishes. She had the dishcloth in her hand. She twisted the red and striped material round and round, only half- hearing his voice. It came out muffled, the way it might as if she needed her ears syringed. She'd had them done once. Afterwards when she opened the newspaper on the bus the rustling sound was like thunder.

He spoke in a quiet voice. 'Life isn't a dress rehearsal,' he said, 'We only get one bite of the cherry. I'll always love you but I'm not *in* love with you.' His voice droned on and on until eventually she got a chance to speak.

She asked if there was someone else. He mumbled about this not being the point. She knew there was. Probably someone much slimmer than she was. He'd been making some remarks about her weight lately. She knew she was putting on a few pounds. She'd even bought one of those 'I Speak Your Weight' machines so she could try and keep it down. She imagined him with a slender young woman in a high-pressure career with a wonderful dress sense.

'You *were* in love with me. Where is that love gone?' she sobbed.

He obviously didn't want to talk about that so he changed the subject. He told her she'd always have the house, and wasn't that a good thing with the mortgage paid and Jack settled now with his own life in Australia. Jack was their son.

'I'll always love you,' he repeated.

'Thanks,' she muttered to herself.

She cried then, big fat splashes of tears rolling down her cheeks. She gave huge gulps because she was trying to stop her nose running. She almost choked trying to swallow the tears. And the snot.

'Look,' he said, 'This can be a new opportunity for you. Women in their fifties are in their prime. Women of your vintage can take their lives in whole new directions. You could even go back to study. Have you ever thought of that? You were always a good reader, right?'

Of course, she thought to herself, who needs men when you can curl up with a good book.

'I'll be perfectly honest,' he went on, 'You're selling yourself short with that trash you read these days. When we met first you were reading Tolstoy and Evelyn Waugh. Now you have your head permanently buried in romantic rubbish. It's doing nothing for your mind, honey. Maybe you could enrol in the Community College and do the Leaving Cert. You're always talking about how you missed out on that. You could even go on to university and take out a degree. You could be a mature student,'

'Is there another woman?' she asked again but he didn't say anything. Because of that, she knew there was. There had to be.

'Has she a degree?' she asked, 'Is she brainy? Does she drive a fancy car? Is she mature?'

'Please,' he said, 'for God's sake, please. I wish you wouldn't go on like this  What's that got to do with anything? Don't beat yourself up with these kinds of questions. The last thing I want to do is hurt you.'

'If you don't want to hurt me,' she said, 'Why are you leaving me? People don't hurt the ones they love.'

'I love you but I'm not *in* love with you.' he said again.

'That's nice to know,' she said. At least he hadn't said, 'It's not you that's the problem, it's me.' That was the usual one. Be thankful for small mercies.

'I don't want to trivialise it,' he said. 'We can love a film, we can love the  cat, we can love steak and onions.  Being *in* love is different. It's exciting.  It changes the whole world.'

'Bully for you,' she said.

'Please, don't make this harder for me than it is,' he pleaded.

'Are you *in* love with this other lady as well as loving her?' she asked, 'Is she more exciting than steak and onions?'

'Please don't be sarcastic,' he said, 'This isn't easy for me.'

'I'm sorry. It's not exactly fun and games for me either.'

'This is getting us nowhere,' he said, 'maybe we can talk when you're calmer.'

'Yes, maybe I can take a Valium and then I'll be feeling on cloud nine.'

She started to cry again. He hated it when she cried. He put his arm around her and she tugged at the expensive lamb's wool jumper she'd bought for him last Christmas. It was maroon, his favourite colour.

'I'm sorry, honey, I really am.'

'Then don't go,' she said.

'But don't you realise – I have to.'

'Why? We've managed up to now. We do have some good times.'

'Yes, but that's in the past. I've been restless for over a year now. I don't know. It's not just you, it's everything. I mean, look around you. Even the house is a mess. I feel a mess myself. We're not eating properly. We're not living properly. We're only half living. Look at the cupboards.'

'I'll clean the cupboards. I'll iron your shirts every Saturday and have them hanging in your wardrobe for the seven days of the week. I'll take lessons in cooking and learn about pasta and stuff they make on telly. I will, I will, please don't go.'

He was at the hall door now. She screamed for him to come back but he didn't look at her. He put on his coat and slammed the door.

She sat on the sofa staring into space. It wasn't the first time he'd gone off in a huff. She'd give him an hour or maybe two to work it off.

106

She looked around at the messy room. She thought of cats and steak and onions and being in love with high pressure career ladies who drove fancy cars.

After a time her tears stopped and she went to the kitchen. She was still clutching the dishcloth. She dried both of their dinner plates and cleaned down the worktop.

The green colour on it was wrong, she thought. It would have been nicer in black marble. He always wanted the black marble. It would have been a better choice. More classy. Maybe if she hadn't been so demanding about the stupid worktop he'd still be 'in' love with her and not thinking about dress rehearsals.

She looked at the clock. He was gone an hour now. Funny that. He usually only stayed out for a half hour or less.

She wiped away the crumbs. Then she got the mop and bucket and scrubbed the floor. The smell was as it said on the bottle, fresh and zingy. Two for the price of one was good value. She put the bucket in its corner and went t into the sitting-room. She set the fire with logs and briquettes. Then she went out to the coal shed and filled the bucket. The handle was very shaky. When he came back she decided she'd ask him to get a new one the next time he was in Woodies. Make him feel important in himself, needed. She never asked him to do anything, that was the problem. Men liked to feel needed.

It would be nice to light the fire, she thought, even though it was only September. She threw some firelighters on it to get it going. As it lit up she decided to iron his shirts and clean out the hot press. He'd be pleased with this when he came back from his walk. He hated clutter and she was the clutterer of the year.

After she ironed the shirts and got the wrinkles out of the collars she sat down and opened herself a bottle of wine. The fire was lighting up really well now. You couldn't beat the few firelighters to get it going.

You're never alone when you have a fire to stare into, she

thought. The wine was going down nicely and the house looked spotless but she kept looking up at the clock. It was over two hours since their little tiff now. He was driving a harder bargain than usual. Maybe she'd have to try harder too. *Not in love,* mind you. Sounded so fancy, didn't it? And all that stuff about dress rehearsals. You'd imagine he was talking about a bloody drama group.

She'd go back to Slim For Life next week and maybe book an appointment to have her hair coloured. The Polish girl made a lovely job of it last time and it was very cheap there. Maybe she'd drop into the library nearby and get some intelligent books as well. He was right - she needed to stimulate her mind. That would please him too.

All that was wrong with their marriage, she realised, was that they were in a bit of a rut. There'd been too much routine lately. Everyone needed some fun. She needed to talk to him about having a break. Italy was supposed to be lovely in October. It might almost act like a second honeymoon.

Two hours turned into three and three into four, five, six. It was now the middle of the night and still no sign of him. That must have been some walk. Where was he going to – China? No, she mustn't make fun of him. He hated that.

Maybe next summer they could visit Jack and his partner Mandy in Australia. Mandy was a nice girl, though a bit standoffish. She'd make a big effort to get to know her. Maybe it was her imagination when she'd heard her talking to Jack during their visit last Christmas. 'Your dad is so interesting,' she'd said, 'but your mum is a little bit dull. Don't get me wrong, Jack, just a little bit.'

She'd cried for two days after that.

She resolved to be different with Mandy when she met her the next time. She'd impress her so much with her cookery classes and her intelligent books. Mandy was a bio-chemist. Such things would be important to her.

Yes, next summer they'd have a get-together, all four of them.

The fire was out now. The bottle was empty. She decided not

to go upstairs tonight. Instead she'd sleep on the sofa.

She was tired. It had been a long day. It was nice to having something to look forward to all the same. A goal in life made all the difference. Australia next year and in October a second honeymoon in Italy. She'd make sure to pack the protection for the sun. Factor 35 for his fair skin but she'd probably get away with the 15.

She was lucky with her colouring. People always admired her sallow complexion. He, on the other hand, had typical Irish skin. At least she had that over him.

She'd book the holiday next week. The weather would be perfect in October and the flights probably more reasonable out of season. Great bargains at that time of the year. They'd sort out everything, she thought. Give them both something to look forward to as well. Italy in October and maybe Australia in the spring.

Every marriage needed a spark. Something to look forward to. That would make all the difference.

# THE MATCHBOX GIRL

I think of my past like gene pools. Like dark, deep water. Holes where generation after generation lie until birth. They climb out and gulp for air eventually. Even Celtic Tigers with botoxed faces and designer handbags have gene pools. Even people in negative equity living on cornflakes. Right back they go through time to slimy creatures who emerged from these holes millions of years ago.

My gene pool is in Galway. The first memory I have of it was the day they gave me a nickname because of a photograph.

'Where's the Matchbox Girl?' Mammy used to say whenever she was looking for me. It was only when I was grown up that I knew why she put that name on me.

I'd been told to stand in front of a matchbox for a school photo. I remember having a stain on my dress. The collar was frayed from scrubbing. My cardigans were in the wash and Mammy had me decked out in a raggedy old jumper. My bumpy knees were banging together, my hands down by my sides.

I was ashamed of the collar sticking out over the jumper. You never wore a jumper over a summer dress. 'Jumpers with fair isle, patterns for winter, everyone knew this, 'little cardigans with beautiful pearl buttons for summer.'

Afterwards I went around the edges of the collar with a blue pen as if that would somehow make it more respectable. I was in High Babies when the picture was taken. Memories of stolen minutes hiding behind the green toilet doors are as real to me as anything that ever happened afterwards.

The picture was from the first school I went to. It was the Irish one at the bottom of Taylor's Hill. My teacher was a big cross woman. She had tight curls in her hair and a red country woman's face. She stood with her bottom up against the fire shouting at us all. We were all terrified of her.

At break times I'd go over and stand at the railings begging Mammy to take me home. Her heart would be broken looking in at me. Then one day she gave in to me, sending me off to the Presentation Convent instead.

It was a better place but I still hated it. Any time away from the classroom was bliss. Maybe I was practising 'mindfulness', as they call it now, living in the now before it became fashionable, before trained members of psychology charged money to train non-members of psychology to 'live in the moment.' (Was it really that hard?)

The 'now' of the classroom was horrible. I felt stupid trying to concentrate on sums. We did adding and subtracting and I could live with those, almost anyway, but then long division came down the track and then algebra, with x and y becoming figures instead of staying in their own place as letters, then geometry with triangles and boxes and a theorem I remember by a man called Pythagoras, I think, that had a big triangle with boxes on each side and one big long one at the bottom. It made a thing called the square on a hypotenuse. I never knew what a hypotenuse was. I kept thinking of Pythagoras in the lavatory. High Pot In Use.

We also had men digging holes, or filling baths, and trains passing each other at certain times and certain speeds and you had to know when they'd pass if they left a certain station at a certain time and I never knew why this should be important, especially if I wasn't on the bloody train, or asked to fill in those big gaping holes.

There were intelligent girls in our classroom who had beautiful names. Heather Flanagan and Antoinette O'Hara asked intelligent questions, their hands waving in the air. 'Me, Sister, me, Sister,' they'd call out, while I tried to put on a serious expression that might make the teacher, a nun I called Pie Face. (Her real name was Sr. Pius). think I knew the answer so she wouldn't ask me and catch me out. I usually hid in the back row, usually in misery but sometimes just staring out the window dreaming.

Pie Face called me Lazarus because I was so sleepy. One day she had to shake me before I even realised she was calling my name from the roll book. Daddy used to try to teach me my sums and he had the patience of a saint. I can still hear him telling me how to do them. 'How many apples would I get for sixpence,' he said, 'if they were two pence each?'

My mind would think of apples with pink juice spurting out of them, This was a time when apples were apples and not manufactured like models in the catwalk all streamlined and flown over from New Zealand or even South Africa. But Daddy never got his answer, or Pie Face either, no matter how much she shook me.

One time I gave my copy to Dolores Connolly. It was one of the few times I got my sums right. I knew they were right because Daddy helped me with them, but me being me I'd done the wrong page.

We were in another room with second class at choir when Pie Face interrupted the class. She called me out with Dolores. She knew Dolores copied me and gave her two slaps with her leather belt. She didn't slap me though, instead telling me I'd have to stay back after class until I had the sums from the right page done correctly.

When I went home for dinner Daddy said we were going to the Silver Strand after school but I had to tell him I was being kept in. He said not to worry, that he'd talk to Pie Face (except he didn't call her that). He came down to the school later and told her about the Silver Strand. Because he was a man she was nice to him and she smiled at me too and told him I was a good girl, even though a bit of a dreamer, and of course that would be grand about the trip to the beach.

Oh, the joy of being let off and knowing I had a daddy who was strong and didn't give one tuppeny damn about Pie Face. We had a great time at the beach but afterwards she paid me back by never asking me even one question for the whole year.

I was glad she didn't ask me sums but there were some things I was good at, like spellings, and she wouldn't ask me them either. I even tried the 'Me, sister! Me, sister! Me, sister!' thing once or twice like Antoinette, waving my hands madly, but it did no good. I was only six then but the hurt of being ignored stayed with me for much of my adult life.

When I moved into first class my life was easier. I was good at English and reading came easy to me. One of the proudest moments of my school life was when I was brought into fifth class to read a piece from their school book. Sister Honoria was a nice nun and she told the big girls to give me a clap.

There were four rows of desks in third class. The sun shone in the window on the Excellent row as if it knew these girls were the Goodie Goodies. Next of all we had the Goods, row Number 2. Then came the Fairs and finally in total darkness the Bads. I was in the Fairs. You could say I wasn't the worst but sometimes I envied the Bads because they didn't care. Or maybe they didn't even know they were classified as being the Bads.

They were the girls who often stayed away on Fridays because they had to help their mothers sell fish,Sister, or who forgot their copybook every single day. Sometimes they seemed above everything. They had a spirit and joy you never saw in the clever madams basking in Sunshine Row.

My day really only began after school. We played cowboys in the lane at the back of our house. There were weeds with little orange circles in them, nettles growing over Miss McHenry's wall, leaves from our garden where we played a game we called Sewing. It consisted of making holes with little sticks and pretending they were stitches. We also played games with tall skinny weeds with brown tops. We had competitions to see who could knock the top off the first. Whoever did was the strongest soldier,

In our turf shed there was a little cave. We played ghost trains there, frightening each other with torn sheets covering our heads. Sometimes myself and Anna Mooney and Mary Reid would go down town and buy sweets you couldn't get in O'Leary's shop, ones shaped like cushions and strong round minty ones. We'd spread them out in saucers and make pretend shops. Jodie Walsh would charge in and turn up the saucers, stuffing the sweets into his mouth. We tried to chase after him but he always got away.

Once I got a bite from Heffernan's greyhound. (I still have the teeth marks on my back). Another time a big boy from Dublin was playing cowboys and Indians with me and the blade flew off the hatchet and I got a huge cut on my forehead. Dr O'Shea had to put seven stitches in it. I still have that mark too.

I had a made-up husband in those days. He was called John. Often when big people came to our house to play cards or sit and talk, Daddy would ask me to tell them about him. I'd ramble on about where John and me were going on our holidays and how he was going to buy me lovely presents. I was going to keep the house spotless for John.

I had a song I made up called 'I'm working from dawn till dust I am, I'm working from dawn till dust.' I don't know where John came from but I felt proud when all the grown-ups would laugh and clap their hands. Timmy Delaney always said 'Where did ye get her, Tom? She's a little pantomime.' Mostly I was shy but when I was doing John it never bothered me if the whole road was watching me.

I loved playing school with younger children and telling them stories. I used to lift them onto our front wall with the twisty pillars and teach them songs or poems. Often they'd knock at our door and say, 'Is Mary is coming out to play?' Mammy would smile at this. One time when Uncle Pat came up from Glenamaddy and I was doing my teaching he said to Mammy 'that girleen will make a great mammy someday.'

I taught Billy Quinn how to spell big long word. The word I chose was 'Difficulty'. I told him the rhyme , 'Mrs D, Mrs I, Mrs FFI, Mrs C, Mrs U, Mrs L, T, Y.' Years later he told me that was the best spelling class he ever had. He remembered it forever He's bald now with a big tummy on him and three grandchildren but it was nice he remembered that.

I loved comics too, especially *School Friend* and *Girl's Crystal*. *School Friend* was in O'Leary's shop on Fridays and *Girl's Crystal* on Wednesdays. Every Christmas they had a lovely album with loads of stories and paper dolls you could cut out and fold cut out dresses on them. There was a girl in the *School Friend* called Sandra and she had a tip tilted nose and a Russian ballet dancer in the *Girl's Crystal* with slanting eyes. I used to stand at the mirror pushing my nose up and trying to pull my eyes sideways thinking this would make me beautiful.

Christmas was my birthday so I got extra treats and Mrs O'Leary from the shop always made me a special birthday Christmas cake with my name in pink writing on the top. On 8th December, a holy day, Mammy and lots of other Mammys would go up to Dublin on the train to do their shopping.

They'd come home on the last train laden down with bags. Mammy would be red in the face with her hair all messy and tell us she was like Biddy Ballymoe. She'd hide the bags because they were out Santy presents but we never ever guessed this.

The best present I ever got was a doll with a beautiful face and brown slanty eyes and a turned up little nose on her. I called her Anita. Her eyes closed when you put her to bed and her golden hair was in ringlets. Afterwards when I was grown out of Santy Mammy told me she had spent Christmas Eve night finishing off the beautiful knitted cape she had made for Anita.

My favourite time of the week was Irish dancing in Mr Fill the Bins kitchen. His real name was Philbin, but we preferred Fill the Bins. He was like a gypsy with dark eyes, like a Spanish person and curly black hair. If you missed a class he'd say, 'And where were you this forty years?' and pretend to be cross. He played the melodeon as well.

He told me I was a topper at dancing the blackbird. I preferred doing the noisy dances like the blackbird, in my hornpipe shoes with the shiny buckles. You could hammer out the beat then, but you wore little pumps for the reels and slip jigs and had to move around the floor so lightly.

One time I won a medal in the Columban Hall for the Blackbird. Mammy did some beautiful embroidery on my cape with Celtic designs. I had a Tara brooch made from a half-crown that a man had made when he was in prison for fighting for Ireland.

I remember the smell of flowers in Lee's front garden. They were pink roses like in granny's garden in Glenamaddy. Then there was the smell of pigs coming from Mr Craven's shed in the back lane, and the smell of rashers and sausages on Sunday mornings after Mass.

What other things come back to me?

Going up to Bishop Brown and asking him could I kiss his ring. Selling him a ticket for a raffle and him giving out to the nuns afterwards about someone as young as me being allowed to do that. Still, the nuns were proud to have the bishop of Galway's name on a ticket, and some important letters after it.

I remember Mammy hiding Jodie Walsh in our house when the guards came to look for him because he stole something. Watching Jodie running down the street with a hen that escaped from the back lane. Listening to Anna Tyrell saying, 'Ana shkins,' which she collected for Cravens pigs. Stealing flowers from Canon Ash's driveway.

Going to the Estoria, or the 'Estore' as we called it, to cowboy pictures with gorgeous ladies washing themselves in tubs while tall cowboys with eyes like the sea peeked a look and told them; 'Lawks Miss Lottie, you sure look purdy when you're riled'. I loved cowboy pictures much more than serious ones and I always shouted for the Apaches to win over them. I even loved the word 'Apache', and Geronimo.

One time myself and poor Anne Lee (we called her 'Anneen') went missing. We wandered away from O'Leary's lane and ended up at the Claddagh. There was a sailor on a boat singing in a foreign language and he asked me to come for a sail with him. I was bending down to go when Anneen pulled me back. Then Mammy and Daddy and loads of other people arrived and marched us home.

Anneen died when she was only 18. She had beautiful curly blond hair and was slender with lovely limbs. She was always rushing to do her wee, hopping frantically from one leg to the other. In school Pie Face gave her a hard time, refusing to let her 'dul amach' when she wanted to go to the toilet. In the end she died from a kidney complaint. Poor Anneen, she was so young.

I went into my own world after she died, imagining fantasies as good as anything I saw in life, or even on the screen. I had a tiny mole between my middle and index finger and I used to examine it when I was lying in bed, thinking to myself, if it ever turns out I'm the daughter of a king they can identify me by that mole. It would be sad leaving Mammy and Daddy and Sean and Maeve but becoming a princess would make up for the loss.

I was never really happy with my name. I was called Mary but I secretly wanted to be called Christina. (I should have been because I was born on Christmas Day). I had fair hair that was parted in the side and came down in what Mammy called a Veronica Lake. I didn't know who Veronica Lake was but I pictured her sitting by a lake combing her long hair. Maybe she was a cousin I thought, but then I discovered she was only a film star and I lost interest in her.

I wanted to be black-haired like my brother and sister. Black was a beautiful colour but fair was just as like its name - fair.

Sean was good at singing. He was called The Wonder Boy Soprano. He used to sing in the Columban Hall. I envied him his voice. Maeve was brainy and could draw beautiful pictures. When she was seven she won a camera in an art competition.

All I had to boast about was my reading. I used to go to the library near the court house every Friday. The first book I ever read was called *Barbara Lamb*. It was about a little lamb that became a singer. She travelled to America and became famous but forgot her friends. They were called Emily Pig and Thomas Donkey.

She put her nose in the air when she became famous. She waved to the crowds dressed in her furs, with diamonds hanging out of her. But then she caught a cold and lost her voice and all her famous important friends ignored her. In the end she was glad to come back to her real friends.

The story was a lesson in how pride can cause a fall but I wasn't bothered about lessons then, I just loved the story. It made a real impression on me and I couldn't stop thinking about it. On trips in the car to see granny and granddaddy in Glenamaddy, every time we passed a field with a lamb in it I'd think it was Barbara. I used to beg Daddy to take her from the field and bring her home to our house.

These things are as real to me now as anything that happened since. What else was there?

Mr O'Leary's ice-cream, the first ever choc ice I ever tasted. It was an Eskimo pie on a stick). Going up Canon Ash's Avenue to steal bluebells and bamboo canes. Having the croup and getting heat treatment from a kettle with a long spout. Water dripping down our green kitchen wall from dampness. Raw chilblains on our fingers and pixies to keep our heads warm. (Daddy always said, 'If you keep your head warm, the rest of you will be grand.')

Mammy used to put ringlets in our hair on Saturday nights. We called them wiggles. We looked like little pickaninnies, Mammy said, with the rags sticking out of our heads. Some girls' mothers put sugar in their hair to make the ringlets harder but our Mammy never did that.

But most of all I remember Uncle Bernie, my mother's brother. Bernie never married. He went bald at 25 and as a result wore a cap all the time. He drank black tea from a cracked white mug and read Westerns with 64 pages in them. I always looked at the back page to see would there be a girl in them. If there wasn't I wouldn't bother reading them.

Bernie was a hackney driver and he let us play in his car when he wasn't using it. It was a big car like no other. Later I heard he got it specially from America. At Christmas and our birthdays he gave us orange ten shilling notes.

When we were older Mammy told us a story about him. One time he fell in love with a girl and bought a house he hoped they could move into on the Kilkerrin Road. But it wasn't to be because she went off with a man from out the country. Afterwards there was only the house. It was empty with dusty windows. When we passed it we peeped through them. We knew it was Bernie's but we also knew we weren't supposed to talk about it. Nobody ever said that to us, we just knew.

When the rest of the family got married, Bernie took care of my grandparents. He also looked after Auntie Bridie who suffered from her nerves. He drove country people to Mass for no pay, just an odd bag of spuds.

He brought Bridie to Castlerea hospital sometimes for electric shock treatment. She'd come home afterwards much quieter but sad as if the shocks had dulled her and shaken the life out of her. At night he'd amble over to Kelly's for a pint, just one pint, and read his Westerns there, or just sit at the counter with his cap on.

The big sadness in our family occurred in January, 1963. My Glenamaddy granny and her oldest child Uncle Miko died at Christmas. There was a piece on the front page of the *Evening Press*: 'Mother and Son Die Within Two Days.' We came to Dublin the following February.

Daddy had been in Dublin since November. He'd been offered a promotion in his job and had to take it. He always refused before but this time he was told that if he refused again he'd never get another offer so he had no choice. We all followed him, leaving St. Mary's Avenue and all our friends, travelling with our bits and pieces into the big unknown.

I asked Uncle Jimmy how many times Dublin was bigger than Galway. 'Hundreds.' he said, 'hundreds bigger than Eyre Square to the end of Salthill, hundreds bigger than all of Shantalla, Taylor's Hill, Dalysfort Road and St. Mary's Avenue.'. I didn't know what hundreds meant. I couldn't take it in.

The night before we left I looked at all the furniture. I said, 'Goodbye kitchen, goodbye sitting-room, goodbye bedrooms, goodbye bathroom, goodbye O'Leary's Lane, goodbye Muddy Starr who made us mittens, goodbye Pat O'Connor whose wife was a lady, goodbye the posh Protestant women and her dogs Spick and Span (or as we called them Dirt and Shtink), goodbye the Pres Convent, goodbye Pie Face, goodbye Tim O'Leary's home-made ice-cream, goodbye Sweet Sixteen, the old woman who wore mini-skirts before they were invented, goodbye Mr Fill the Bin, goodbye Anna Tyrell, goodbye Anneen Lee, goodbye Billy Quinn, goodbye Billy Barrett who tied my ribbon for me on Canon Ash's Avenue, goodbye, goodbye, goodbye.

And so we moved to the house in Artane. It was on a wide road with nothing but concrete in it. There was no Monk's field, no greenness at all, just every house with cross-looking windows covered up with stripey Venetian blinds that I absolutely hated. I looked around me at the new roads, the dug-up little gardens, the bare whiteness of it all. I felt like one of those weeds with the lovely orange balls that was yanked from the warm delicious smelly place near Craven's pig shed and transported up to a cold hard stony place.

The rooms were all painted cream. We opened all the doors we could find, checking out everything. Our couch looked old and shabby in the living-room. Our kitchen table was like something from a dump. The smart white rooms seemed to me to be looking at our possessions in disgust. Mammy stacked the delph in fitted cupboards, our lovely green dresser being too old to travel.

Daddy told us there was a supermarket just around the corner. 'If you get some milk and tea for now,' Mammy said, 'We can leave the big shopping till tomorrow.'

Maeve and myself went out onto the strange road. There was a girl skipping outside the house next door. 'Let's pretend we have posh names,' I said to Maeve, 'You can be Cynthia and I'll be Anita, just like the girls in *School Friend*.'

We stood watching the girl. Maeve had her glasses on. The girl stared at us. We stared back.

'Well,' she said, 'Have yez seen enough, Specky Four Eyes?'

'Shut up,' said Maeve.

'   Don't mind her,' I said, 'She has no manners.'

She gave a big laugh when she heard our accents.

'Jaysus,' she said, 'two bleedin' culchies. Just my luck.'

We went off to the shops but on the way back we couldn't decide which side of the road our house was because they all looked the same.

'Dublin is a stupid place,' I said when we finally saw the hall door. It was number 74.

When we went in, mammy made a cup of tea. We listened to the rasp of the kettle and then it bubbled over. Mammy reached into the strange cabinet for our old Galway cups. She made us tea but it tasted funny.

Afterwards we tried to turn on the television but it wouldn't work so we just sat around trying to talk instead. None of us had much to say. We were all too sad but we didn't want to admit it. We tried to put on bright faces but nobody was convinced.

When we went to bed I couldn't sleep for hours. I thought of a boy in a story Daddy read to me once who had a 'pain in his belly with the lonesome.' I cried as I listened to the cars moving up and down the road and the big noisy trucks. Maeve was awake too so we decided to play a game. We called it 'Stall.' That  was our short way of saying 'Stay Awake All Night.' We drifted off after a while but when I woke up the next morning I felt even more miserable.

Eventually we settled into our Dublin home. Mammy stashed away her black mourning clothes and had her hair permed.  Daddy put flowery wallpaper in the hall to cover up the horrible cold whiteness. We even gave in and got the dreaded Venetian blinds eventually because everyone else had them. You had to. It was now the sixties and nobody was anything without them.

School was even more horrible for me in Dublin. We had to wear indoor shoes and have our hair tied back at all times. More girls than our neighbour laughed at my culchie accent. I was still useless at sums and even worse at sports. I hated the hockey pitch especially. Big hefty popular girls with huge thighs terrified me and eventually I was excused from playing. I had to spend games time reading holy books with two other misfits.

I battled on until the Inter Cert. My marks were low except for an honour I got in English. Then Daddy agreed to take me out of school. Maeve and Sean went on to graduate with good grades but I 'just' became a shorthand typist.

The years after that time are bundled together in my mind. I moved through life thinking of nothing but the moment. I can't remember what I did either in work or out of work. I was in my own head a lot of the time. I made up fantasies reading books and going to cowboy films – at least if they had romances in them.

Maeve got married when she was 21. She's a grandmother now, well settled and living in County Offaly. Sean lives in London. He divorced his English wife and is with an Irish girl now. They come home at Christmas and stay with Maeve. I only see them every few years.

I had one or two relationships of my own. I almost married a teacher when I was in my early thirties but it fizzled out, probably because we had so little in common. Maybe I wasn't the marrying kind, or was it just didn't meet the right man?

Daddy and Mammy are dead over thirty years now. Uncle Bernie died in the Regional in Galway. When I visited him in 1977 when he was very ill he was plugged into a machine. He was lying on a narrow bed with his poor bald head exposed to bustling nurses and important-looking doctors. I thought of his cowboy books, the mugs of black tea he drank and his lonely bare house. I wanted to drag him from that sterile world and let him die in peace with his cap on, dragging the last out of another Sweet Afton cigarette, his head buried in a story from the wild, wild west.

Next year I'll be retiring. They'll give me a lump sum and a weekly pension and maybe a voucher from the One for All from the Post Office. These vouchers are much more useful than the ones that only allow you to buy from one shop only. You can even use them towards your weekly groceries.

I'll put the 'lump' in a deposit account and live on the pension. It's sensible to have something put aside because we all know big sums of money dwindle to nothing if you keep dipping into them. I might splurge out and get the house decorated. Wallpaper is too old-fashioned so I think I'll have all the rooms painted instead. The colour I've decided on is cream. Cream always looks good.

The Venetian blinds are getting very shabby now. They owe me nothing. Maybe I'll wander into Arnott's and get some good quality curtains. A heavy brocade material always looks the money. I could put the One For All vouchers towards them.

I'll have to be careful because the pension will be huge drop from my salary but I think I'll manage. I know Daddy would be pleased with me if he was alive today. He always thought I was living in the clouds. I was but I'm not anymore.

I budget well now. My bills are paid on time and I've got better at Maths too. How long it takes men to dig holes or trying to figure out what time trains pass each other travelling at certain speeds doesn't really matter. Managing your money is what it's all about. When you think of it, the secret of a happy life is learning to live within your means. That's my philosophy anyway.

Sometimes when I look at that faded picture of me I see the girl I was when I stood behind the matchbox. I think of the dreams I had then, I think of John, my make-believe husband, I think of the children I played games with, I think of Barbara Lamb, I think of sewing on leaves.

I wonder about the meaning of life too, of course, but wondering never got the bills paid, did it?

All my memories are still important to me but age has brought me a different perspective on things. I see my memories as being a bit silly now. Why did I hate Venetian blinds when they're so practical? Why was I so against Dublin when there are so many facilities here, so many things in the shops that you can't get in Galway or the smaller towns of Ireland?

Billy Quinn is bald now. Billy Barrett is dead. It's not healthy to think about people like that. What good is it trying to romanticise a disappeared past? What good can it do me when I have the hard present to contend with?

Marriage passed me by but that's no regret of mine when I see so many marriages of my friends breaking up because their husbands cheated on them.

If I went off with the sailor that day in the Claddagh, would it have worked out? Would a marriage with my pretend husband have worked out? Would he have been a cheater too? Maybe he'd have gone off with a younger woman when I started to show my ag, or went grey. Or maybe he'd have got fat and bald like Billy Quinn or died like Billy Barrett. They say loneliness is much worse for people who've been married than the ones who never knew what it was like to have a Significant Other in their lives.

'If it isn't for you it'll pass you by,' a friend of mine said to me recently. I think she's right. We have to jolly up and get on with things.

The past may be beautiful but it's gone. At the end of the day it's no more use to us than leaves pressed into an old photograph album. It's as dead as the leaves themselves and a danger to us as we press forward to whatever future we might be lucky enough to find.

# Narcisismo en español/ Narcissism in Spanish

*Comprender el trastorno de la personalidad narcisista*

El siguiente libro se reproduce a continuación con el objetivo de proporcionar información lo más precisa y confiable posible. En cualquier caso, la compra de este libro puede considerarse como un consentimiento al hecho de que tanto el editor como el autor de este libro no son expertos en los temas tratados y que las recomendaciones o sugerencias que se hacen en este documento son solo para fines de entretenimiento. Los profesionales deben ser consultados según sea necesario antes de emprender cualquiera de las acciones aquí mencionadas.

Esta declaración se considera justa y válida tanto por Colegio de Abogados de América como por el Comité de la Asociación de Editores y es legalmente vinculante en todos los Estados Unidos.

Además, la transmisión, duplicación o reproducción de cualquiera de los siguientes trabajos, incluida información específica, se considerará un acto ilegal independientemente de si se realiza de forma electrónica o impresa. Esto se extiende a la creación de una copia secundaria o terciaria del trabajo o una copia grabada y solo se permite con el consentimiento expreso por escrito del Editor. Todos los derechos adicionales reservados.

La información en las siguientes páginas se considera, en términos generales, como una descripción veraz y precisa de los hechos y, como tal, cualquier falta de atención, uso o mal uso de la información en cuestión por parte del lector hará que las acciones resultantes sean únicamente de su competencia. No hay escenarios en los que el editor o el autor original de este trabajo puedan ser considerados responsables de cualquier dificultad o daño que pueda ocurrirles después de realizar la información aquí descrita.

Además, la información en las siguientes páginas está destinada únicamente a fines informativos y, por lo tanto, debe considerarse como universal. Como corresponde a su naturaleza, se presenta sin garantía con respecto a su validez prolongada o calidad provisional. Las marcas comerciales que se mencionan se realizan sin consentimiento por escrito y de ninguna manera pueden considerarse un respaldo del titular de la marca comercial.

# Tabla de Contenido

# Introducción

Felicitaciones por descargar *Narcisismo: Comprender el trastorno de la personalidad narcisista* y gracias por hacerlo.

Los siguientes capítulos discutirán el peligro muy real de acercarse a un narcisista. Actualmente, el narcisismo es una palabra de moda tan popular que puede ser difícil discernir los "rasgos narcisistas" del narcisismo maligno real. Casi todo el mundo conoce a alguien que muestra rasgos de arrogancia, egoísmo y que ama estar en el centro de atención, pero ¿cómo sabe si realmente se encuentra cara a cara con un narcisista?

Discutiremos las diversas tácticas y técnicas que el narcisista emplea para mantener a sus víctimas sometidas y bajo control, y sin saber realmente cuál es la realidad y qué es una ilusión. También se discutirán términos tales como *"hacer luz de gas", proyección, tergiversación y generalización radical, y congelamiento.*

Cubriremos la dinámica de una familia narcisista y cómo esa estructura puede ser el núcleo más devastador para los niños. Es importante saber cómo protegerse y proteger a sus seres queridos si se encuentra en un tira y encoge con un narcisista, ya sea un miembro de la familia, cónyuge o padre. Una vez que reconoce los signos de narcisismo en la dinámica familiar, puede tomar medidas para que usted y sus seres queridos lleguen a orillas más seguras y comience también el proceso de sanación.

Este libro le revelará los diferentes tipos de narcisistas y discutirá teorías sobre cómo podría llegar a ser el narcisismo en un individuo. También detallará el abuso emocional y mostrará las comparaciones entre una relación sana y una tóxica. Desglosará el proceso de sanación del abuso emocional y qué esperar cuando intenta separarse de la red enredada de un narcisista.

Hay muchos libros sobre este tema en el mercado, ¡gracias de nuevo por elegir este! Se hizo todo lo posible para garantizar que esté lleno de tanta información útil como sea posible, ¡por favor, disfrute!

# Capítulo 1: ¿Qué es el Narcisismo?

El Narcisismo es una palabra bastante popular en este momento. Innumerables gurús de autoayuda, grupos de redes sociales, páginas de memes, artículos de HuffPost y Buzzfeed nos dicen qué observar si nos cruzamos con estos presuntos monstruos presumidos de selfies, orgullosos, pretenciosos y jactanciosos. Pero, ¿tomarse una selfie es una indicación de algo más siniestro bajo la superficie, o todos nos hemos convertido en víctimas de la exageración, viendo monstruos en cada sombra?

Mi padre me dijo una vez que está bien ser egoísta. No era, de hecho, un narcisista.

Explicó que estaba mirando la palabra desde una definición única (y que no encontrará en el diccionario). Explicó que preocuparse por uno mismo, poner el yo primero en la mayoría de las situaciones no es necesariamente algo malo. Aquí es donde nos detenemos y observamos qué es realmente el narcisismo, primero examinando qué *no es el narcisismo.*

Tomemos a los adolescentes, por ejemplo. Sería difícil hacer que el adolescente promedio mire más allá de sí mismo en muchas situaciones. Están obsesionados con su apariencia externa y las opiniones de los demás sobre ellos. Están atrapados en un intenso estado de crisálida para descubrir quiénes son y eso requiere mucho autoexamen. Es difícil ver el mundo que le rodea cuando se está mirando al espejo todo el tiempo.

Sin embargo, tome a ese adolescente promedio, cuando no esté mirando su teléfono celular para otra selfie, y colóquelo en una posición en la que alguien esté en apuros evidentes, justo en frente de ellos. Puede que no sepan qué hacer o decir, puede que no sepan cómo actuar o incluso cómo ayudar, pero incluso si no hicieron nada en absoluto, si les preguntaran sobre el momento, más adelante, es probable que al responder, desmuestre que al menos, el adolescente sintió empatía hacia la persona en peligro.

*Aquí* es donde la autoabsorción y el narcisismo se separan porque el narcisista no puede sentir empatía, hacia nadie, bajo ninguna circunstancia.

¿Cómo se convierte uno en narcisista? ¿Qué le sucede a una persona y cuándo, de repente, eso le quita la empatía, un rasgo directamente relacionado con nuestra humanidad? Varios factores, algunos de los cuales ocurren en los años formativos de un niño, pueden contribuir al desarrollo del narcisismo. La genética y las anormalidades de la estructura del cerebro pueden contribuir al narcisismo. Además, la dinámica de un hogar infantil puede dificultar el crecimiento de la empatía, como la crianza psicológicamente insalubre. Antes de preguntarse si ha marcado a su propio hijo para un futuro de narcisismo, recuerde esto: todos los padres cometen errores y ningún padre es perfecto. Sin embargo, las probabilidades son muy buenas de que a lo largo de su relación con su hijo o hijos, haya mostrado empatía por ellos y, al hacerlo, les haya enseñado la valiosa y esencial lección de que la empatía nos conecta a todos.

Sin embargo, un narcisista no necesariamente obtuvo esa importante lección.

Quizás sus padres los criaron dentro de un exceso de falsos elogios. Si bien los niños *necesitan* elogios para prosperar, un entorno en el que literalmente nunca han hecho nada malo es increíblemente tóxico para ellos y les lleva a un sentido inflado de importancia personal. El arte de ser humilde es esencial para el crecimiento personal, para la conexión con los demás, incluso para una mayor confianza en uno mismo. Imagine a un niño que cree que es perfecto al encontrarse con su primer crítico. Para un narcisista, la crítica es inaceptable y a menudo desencadena episodios de ira o venganza.

En casos raros, el narcisismo puede brotar como defensa propia contra una abundancia de crueldad durante la infancia; en esencia, la exposición al narcisismo genera más narcisismo.

Cualquiera que sea el caso, cuando una figura parental está completamente fuera de tono con la realidad de su hijo, esa figura le enseña una y otra vez que la realidad del niño no existe. Los narcisistas no sienten amor por sí mismos, no pueden producir alegría propia. La formación de autoestima y autocuidado estuvo completamente ausente, mientras que sus cerebros en crecimiento aprendieron una y otra vez que el único camino hacia la satisfacción en la vida, era a través de la manipulación de los demás, y este extracción de las experiencias de los demás se llama suministro narcisista.

Un narcisista mantendrá a una o más víctimas (que incluso podemos llamarlas extensiones y que el narcisista las usará como un parásito) cerca, instalándose rápidamente en la vida de las víctimas y con grandes promesas de conexión, respeto y la más importante, admiración. El narcisista sabe cómo mentir porque le han mentido toda su vida por aquellos que se suponía que lo protegerían, y puede ser bastante encantador cuando eso significa aumentar su suministro.

El narcisista manipulará a los que están a su disposición para proporcionarle entretenimiento, aliento, una distracción básica y primaria que le impide mirar hacia adentro, porque si mira hacia adentro, básicamente está mirando al vacío.

Aquellos particularmente vulnerables a los comportamientos del narcisista son aquellos que, naturalmente, sienten la mayor cantidad de empatía por los demás. Debido a que estas personas hacen que sea mucho más fácil para el narcisista proyectar, son el objetivo número uno.

Mientras tanto, el narcisista está manipulando a las personas más cercanas a él, no se da cuenta de que lo está haciendo. La necesidad de alimentarse de la angustia de los demás está tan arraigada, tan subconsciente, que sugerirle algo más que lo ordinario, es desencadenar aún más medidas defensivas. Liberarse de un narcisista implicará muchas amenazas, mucho sabotaje y más de un retroceso, ya que el narcisista tratará de reconstruir esa conexión; después de todo, si pierde una conexión, significa que ha fallado, y dado que es imposible que falle, debe intentar recuperar todo lo que ha perdido, a toda costa.

Las herramientas en el kit de un narcisista incluyen cosas tales como "hacer luz de gas", redirección, proyección, distorsión, junto con un talento para la actuación que le otorgaría a cualquiera un Oscar en un papel secundario. El narcisista ha visto a las personas mostrar empatía y preocupación reales y sabe cómo imitarlo cuando las cosas se ponen difíciles. Eso no cambia el hecho de que no tienen idea de cómo sentir realmente estas cosas; es como si le preguntaras a uno un pez, cómo es respirar aire.

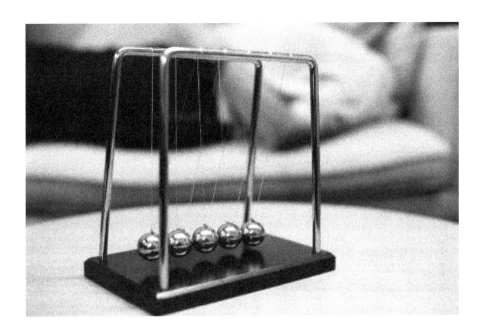

## Narcisismo en acción

Una forma simplificada de ver el narcisismo es comprender que, en esencia, un narcisista tiene problemas para escuchar a los demás. No estamos hablando de problemas de déficit de atención aquí: un narcisista escucha palabras, claro, pero a medida que pasan de la boca del orador a los oídos del narcisista, se traducen en: *Te estoy ignorando. Te estoy aburriendo. Estoy perdiendo tu tiempo. Estoy quebrantando tu importancia.*

Esto, por supuesto, es inaceptable, porque el narcisista es lo más importante del mundo, para sí mismo.

Uno puede ver rápidamente la encantadora fachada del narcisista derrumbarse en ira, incluso desprecio, si la persona a la que está escuchando dice algo que no le gusta o le resulta aburrido, o el cielo no lo permita, es cualquier tipo de crítica hacia el narcisista. Eso se convierte en un ataque directo.

Además, esa falta de empatía se traduce en una forma brutal de tratar con las personas cercanas al narcisista. El sarcasmo constante desgasta a sus seres queridos, erosionando la autoestima y la confianza en sí mismo. El narcisista jugará juegos de felicidad y odio, donde en un momento el narcisista se alegra de la compañía de su víctima, y luego al otro momento, desaparece, tiene un trato silencioso o descarga un aluvión de comportamiento violento y abusivo como expresión de disgusto.

## Trastorno de personalidad narcisista versus narcisismo simple

Puede ser difícil discernir las diferencias entre el narcisismo promedio y corriente y el NPD real, que se clasifica como una enfermedad mental.

El narcisismo como rasgo de la personalidad está bastante extendido. La arrogancia, la jactancia, el sentido excesivamente inflado de importancia se pueden ver en nuestra sociedad, desde los CEO de las principales corporaciones hasta la política, el atletismo y las celebridades. Todo esto llega a la persona común; Si funciona para el éxito salvaje, ¿por qué no funcionaría para el vecino?

Cuando un individuo tiene problemas para tratar con otros; cuando tienen problemas para enfrentar sus situaciones emocionales; cuando tienen dificultades para mantener relaciones saludables o incluso poder discernir qué es una relación saludable, es entonces cuando una personalidad narcisista promedio cruza la frontera hacia una enfermedad mental real.

En general, los psicólogos coinciden en que este tipo más extremo de narcisismo no es causado o desencadenado por el abuso de sustancias, factores externos o el medio ambiente. Viene dentro y crece más maligno cada día.

## La diferencia entre el trastorno de la personalidad narcisista y el trastorno límite de la personalidad

Estos dos trastornos a menudo se confunden entre sí, pero existen diferencias importantes. Primero, el trastorno límite de la personalidad, o TLP, se produce como resultado directo del entorno de una persona, especialmente a una edad temprana. El trauma repetido a través del abuso o la dinámica familiar tumultuosa y centrada en la ira, puede con el tiempo, dar como resultado que una persona desarrolle patrones de comportamiento como mecanismo de defensa contra la interrupción futura. Estos patrones de comportamiento son los que marcan la imagen clásica de alguien que sufre de TLP.

Las personas con TLP a menudo tienen tremendos problemas de abandono, derivados de la falta de conexión o el abandono absoluto cuando eran niños. Creen que todos los amigos los abandonarán. Algunos incluso tienen problemas para despedirse de un compañero cuando ese compañero sale por la puerta del trabajo. Atacarán, actuarán e incluso se lanzarán a lastimar a sus seres queridos cuando el miedo a ser lastimados aumente. Irónicamente, a menudo alejan a las personas o huyen de las relaciones debido a este mismo miedo al abandono.

Sin embargo, la diferencia entre alguien con TLP y alguien con NPD es que la persona que padece TLP sentirá remordimiento y vergüenza por sus comportamientos. Pueden tomar conciencia de sus ciclos de dolor e incluso tomar medidas para romper esos ciclos y así poder controlar mejor su comportamiento reactivo. Con el tiempo, una persona con TLP puede incluso "vencer" el comportamiento sintomático, convirtiéndose en alguien que ya no es esclavo de sus propios temores de abandono y abuso.

Sin embargo, una persona con NPD simplemente no puede percibir las consecuencias de su comportamiento en términos de dañar a otra persona. La empatía no está ahí. Saben lo que lastimará a alguien, y utilizarán ese conocimiento para obtener lo que desean, y no sienten remordimiento alguno por tomar esas decisiones. Hay muchos que dicen que debido a esto, el verdadero NPD nunca se puede sanar o salir de allí.

Las personas con trastorno de personalidad narcisista también albergan temores extremos de abandono. Sin embargo, su forma de tratarlo es marcadamente diferente a la de aquellos que tienen TLP. El narcisista se esfuerza por mantener a las personas cerca de ellos a través del abuso sistémico y el desprendimiento regular de la realidad.

Tanto aquellos con NPD como con TLP, tienen muchas cosas en común. Ambos operan en una especie de ciclo. Aquellos con NPD se acercan a las personas que utilizan primero una "fase encantadora", que se sirve de cumplidos y atención en un esfuerzo por atraer a esa persona para que se acerque a ellos. Las personas con TLP vuelven este encanto como un foco de luna de miel hacia adentro: "idealizan" a la nueva persona, colocándola en un pedestal, como si nadie más en el mundo pudiera ser comparado con ellos.

La siguiente fase también es similar para ambos. El narcisista comenzará a desglosar las defensas y la realidad de la persona "encantada", utilizando trucos y técnicas que discutiremos más adelante en este libro. Esa persona pasará de creer que el narcisista fue lo mejor que les ha pasado, a preguntarse por qué todavía se queda cuando el narcisista los encuentra tan horribles.

(Pista: el narcisista no los encuentra geniales, ni horribles, sino necesarios).

Por otro lado, la persona que padece TLP llegará a un punto en el tiempo, en que el objeto de su adoración comete un error, y este error causará la fase devastadora en la que la persona con TLP ve que su perfección se derrumba. El antiguo objeto de su devoción se ve a través de un lente oscuro sobre dramático. Nunca fueron buenos, nunca se preocuparon por la persona, sus intenciones siempre fueron cuestionables, por lo que la persona con TLP se retira.

La capacidad simple de escuchar simultáneamente los pensamientos, sentimientos e inquietudes de otra persona, al tiempo que puede expresar los suyos de una manera objetiva y no destructiva, no es simple ni está disponible para aquellos que sufren de NPD y TLP: la diferencia es a través de la terapia y la fuerza de voluntad, el paciente con TLP puede evolucionar para dominar la capacidad de comunicación y asociación saludables. El paciente con NPD no puede.

# Capítulo 2: Abuso Narcisista

Los narcisistas no suelen ser personas felices, no del mismo modo que todos los demás son felices. Entre su ser construido como una fachada y la realidad de la profunda vergüenza, albergan dentro de sí mismos una gran brecha. Necesitan distraerse constantemente del dolor de esta existencia abusando de otros y obteniendo las reacciones de los demás de ese abuso. Esa reacción se conoce como *suministro narcisista.*

**Pueden invadir su privacidad.** Un narcisista puede revisar sus correos electrónicos y su teléfono, mirar a través de su correo, revisar los cajones en busca de secretos que les haya ocultado (o, en realidad, cosas que aún no ha decidido compartir con ellos). Pueden revisar los textos en su teléfono y sacar conclusiones irracionales y exageradas de ellos. Pueden buscar en la web cosas relacionadas con su nombre, ver quién respondió a sus publicaciones e imágenes en las redes sociales, así como ver los perfiles de las personas a las que está conectado en las redes sociales.

**Fría hostilidad.** Puede notar que incluso cuando un narcisista le dice cosas bonitas, su cabello se eriza, hay un escalofrío en el aire. Los cumplidos, las charlas alentadoras, las expresiones de apoyo y las confesiones de amor, todo esto se siente extremadamente incorrecto, como si el narcisista hubiera recibido un guión. La realidad es que estas palabras, por bonitas que sean en el exterior, son realmente métodos de manipulación. Aquellos que han sido criados en tales entornos generalmente son incapaces de reconocer estas técnicas en las relaciones adultas.

**El narcisista puede descuidar a sus seres queridos.** Los niños que crecen con padres narcisistas recordarán que los dejaron solos o ignorados cuando se lesionaron o enfermaron.

**Retención como castigo.** El narcisista puede mantener el dinero, la atención, el tiempo, el sexo, incluso la conversación informal (también conocido como trato silencioso) como un medio para herir a sus seres queridos o tomar represalias contra los desaires o ataques percibidos.

**Un narcisista puede explotarlo o aprovecharse de usted** por diversión o por sus propias necesidades. Para un narcisista, usted no es una persona real y no le importa. Existe dentro de su círculo interno para satisfacer sus necesidades, nada más.

**Con frecuencia pueden compararte** con ellos mismos u otros. Esto es importante de reconocer. Una persona psicológicamente sana, rara vez pide a alguien que la compare con otra persona porque saben que todos son únicos y que realmente no hay tal cosa como ser "mejor" o "peor" que nadie. Todos tenemos nuestros propios talentos únicos, luchas, rasgos negativos. Por lo tanto, ser comparado con otras personas, o con la narcisista misma, desgastará regularmente a la víctima del abuso, y quejarse de ello o intentar luchar contra él, solo empeorará las cosas.

**Le resultará difícil lograr el éxito personal** en cualquier área de su vida porque el narcisista se tomará ese éxito personalmente. Por lo tanto, el narcisista intentará sabotearlo de cualquier manera que pueda. Puede mentirle a sus amigos o tratar de convencerlo de que las probabilidades son demasiado grandes para que tenga éxito, por lo que debe rendirse. Especialmente cuando se trata de otras relaciones, ya sea con amigos, compañeros de trabajo, familiares, el narcisista también intentará sabotearlas. Cuanto más cerca esté el narcisista de convertirse en el centro de su mundo, más fácil será para esa persona manipularle y obtener suministros de usted.

**La mentira y el engaño constantes** ayudan al narcisista a distorsionar sistemáticamente su sentido de la realidad. Es difícil contraatacar cuando ya ni siquiera sabe quién es usted, o incluso si es el que comete el abuso, ya que un narcisista intentará convencerlo.

**Una cosa tan simple como jugar un juego**, ya sea ajedrez, cartas, un juego de mesa, un videojuego multijugador revelará la verdadera naturaleza de un narcisista. Pueden hacer trampa o usar tácticas altamente agresivas que están perfectamente dentro de las reglas pero aseguran que el narcisista siempre gane, siempre salga adelante. No hay tal cosa como jugar por diversión. Cada ejercicio y práctica en la vida diaria debe servir para destacar cuán mejor es el narcisista que todos los demás. Si alguien más parece que podría ganar el juego, los jugadores corren el riesgo de desencadenar un episodio de ira narcisista: puede barrer el tablero de la mesa, puede arrojar los vasos contra las paredes, los invitados se van apurados, avergonzados e incómodos, y el compañero del narcisista irse con una noche muy larga y dolorosa, tal vez hasta el amanecer.

**El chantaje emocional** es una táctica utilizada por los narcisistas para armar a su pareja para que haga lo que el narcisista quiere que haga. Si la pareja finalmente ha decidido terminar la relación y marcharse, por ejemplo, el narcisista puede decir que planea suicidarse si la pareja se va. El narcisista también puede tratar de intimidar a su pareja o amenazarla: si la pareja está atrapada en sentimientos de dolor, tristeza, traición, desesperanza, entonces está completamente al antojo y llamado del narcisista y no puede reunir la energía para luchar adecuadamente o irse.

**Hacer luz de gas** a menudo seguirá o precederá al chantaje emocional. El término Hacer luz de gas o Gaslighting proviene de una obra originalmente llamada Angel Street, pero cambió el nombre de Gas Light cuando se convirtió en una película, en la que un personaje hace pequeñas cosas para convencer a su pareja de que están locos, como mover cosas por la casa y negar conversaciones que sucedieron. Un narcisista negará, evadirá o redirigirá constantemente los momentos de la realidad para que, con el tiempo, su pareja se cuestione constantemente. Una táctica que usan los compañeros es grabar conversaciones, pero esto también desencadenará un episodio de ira narcisista. El narcisista nunca debe ser confrontado con su propio comportamiento; son incapaces de asumir la culpa por el dolor de otra persona.

Otras razones por las que un narcisista hace luz de gas, es para que su pareja se sienta incompetente o incluso afectada por un trastorno de personalidad. Toda acusación u observación, sin importar cuán diplomáticamente expresada sea o cuán objetiva, se dará la vuelta y se usará, eventualmente para acusar al acusador.

Las tácticas para mantenerlo conectado a su realidad bajo un asalto directo a la luz de gas incluyen escribir cosas, compartir los momentos con amigos confiables e incluso publicar momentos en las redes sociales, siempre y cuando estén lejos de las miradas indiscretas del narcisista. Recuerde, nunca podrá demostrar su valía ante el narcisista; lo que intenta hacer es demostrarse a usted mismo que estos momentos ocurrieron para que se mantenga firme en su realidad.

**El sarcasmo** es el idioma que más hablan los narcisistas. Nunca habrá un cumplido u observación honestos sin un tono más oscuro de sarcasmo entretejido. El compañero del narcisista nunca debe sentirse seguro, nunca sentirse lo suficientemente bueno, aunque en el período encantador, se les podría haber dicho: *"Te elegí porque eras digno"*. Ahora que la persona es un elemento permanente en la vida del narcisista, es más probable que escuche *"Sí claro...eres un buen arquitecto"*, con un sarcasmo tan mordaz que parece capaz de cortar la piel.

**Proyección.** Esta es una de las herramientas que utiliza un narcisista para mantenerlo en pie y evitar que pueda determinar la realidad de la ilusión. Si alguna vez usted se atreve a acusar al narcisista de algo, incluso si solo está sugiriendo que puede ser una posibilidad, espere a que las cosas cambien cuando el narcisista lo acuse de lo mismo. Puede que no sea inmediato, pero se sorprenderá al escuchar sus propias acusaciones contra usted, a veces palabra por palabra, cuando se produce la proyección.

**Tergiversación y generalizaciones radicales.** El arsenal del narcisista está fuertemente acribillado con el hábito de inclinar la cordura de arrojarle grandes declaraciones, como *"siempre eres infeliz"* o *"si fueras un hombre de verdad, tú..."* Una vez que el narcisista haya adquirido un conjunto de cosas para etiquetarle, las usará para descartar todo lo que tenga que decir. Con el tiempo, se convertirán en microagresiones, una cancelación de su individualidad, su ser y su identidad. Simplemente se convertirá en la persona que el narcisista dice que es.

Además, el narcisista responderá a sus declaraciones o preguntas con declaraciones ridículas propias. Si durante una conversación sobre los años universitarios, admite que finalmente ha sido feliz consigo mismo, su compañero narcisista podría responder de repente: *"¿Entonces ahora eres perfecto?"* O incluso más incomprensiblemente: *"Entonces, supongo que soy un pedazo de basura entonces"*. No hay conexión de los puntos en una conversación con un narcisista. Como regla, muchos de ellos son pensadores perezosos porque sus frágiles egos no pueden manejar grandes hazañas de análisis. No pueden manejar la autorreflexión porque detestan lo que ven. Entonces, para ellos, la vida se convierte en una serie de extrañas declaraciones generales que a menudo no parecen encajar en el contexto de la conversación en la que se insertan.

**Lectura de la mente.** Otra de las tácticas recurrentes del narcisista es creer que lo conocen mejor que usted mismo (y usarán esa línea constantemente). Esta es una forma de socavar su autoridad y sentido de sí mismo, pero también para cerrar conversaciones que no quieren tener.

Sobre cosas tan simples como elegir una camisa en una tienda, si el narcisista quiere elegir este momento para lastimarlo, lo hará. *"Crees que te ves bien en estampados, pero sabes que solo te hace ver más gordo. Piensas que estás en forma pero no lo estás"*. Cosas como esta a menudo se dicen frente a otras personas para agregar impacto al golpe.

**Portería en movimiento.** A un narcisista no le importa si usted tiene éxito en la vida. Su éxito puede haber sido una de las cosas que atrajo al narcisista hacia usted, ya sea porque demostró que era digno de su compañía, o porque se convirtió en un desafío para el narcisista desanimarlo, o incluso porque significaba que el narcisista llegó a competir usted, pero una vez que está en una relación con un narcisista, su éxito es solo un desafío, un aburrimiento y/o una amenaza para los logros del narcisista. El narcisista puede fingir que lo está apoyando, pero una vez que logra algo que ha estado intentando durante un tiempo, el narcisista se dará vuelta y mencionará un objetivo más elevado, y borrará completamente el momento de su éxito en el ahora.

Con el tiempo, el mensaje subconsciente que le envía el narcisista es que no es lo suficientemente bueno y nunca lo será. Una y otra vez, intenta complacer a su pareja narcisista, pero con el tiempo, se dará cuenta de que nada de lo que haga, puede cambiar su comportamiento abusivo. Nunca se puede ganar el favor de un narcisista porque un narcisista solo se favorece a sí mismo.

**Profundizando en tonterías.** Las conversaciones y discusiones con un narcisista a menudo van de lo sublime a lo ridículo. Si comete el error de señalar que su compañero narcisista debería prestar más atención a sus hijos, el narcisista podría mencionar un error que cometió hace cinco años, y uno que bien podría no tener nada que ver con el tema de conversación en cuestión. No hay rima ni razón para tratar de razonar con un narcisista. Usarán lo que esté a la mano, cualquier cosa que sea, para deshabilitarlo o disuadirlo de querer seguir hablando en voz alta. Para un narcisista, nunca hay paz.

**Ira narcisista.** Cuando un narcisista percibe un desaire o un ataque, con bastante frecuencia puede desencadenarlo en algo llamado ira narcisista. Aquí todo es posible. Recurrirán a insultos, amenazas de represalias románticas, violencia física, amenazas a la familia y sus pertenencias. Incluso si retrocede, el castigo continuará, a menudo enfriándose hasta el silencio o el abandono durante días, incluso semanas a la vez.

Además de los insultos, el narcisista a menudo comenzará a desglosar sus creencias, su identidad, su fe y su conjunto de habilidades, cualquier cosa que sea única y personal para usted, de modo que con el tiempo comience a sentirse como una farsa, un farsante, digno de nada más que burla. En este estado, no puede representar una amenaza o una molestia para un narcisista, pero puede proporcionar horas y horas de entretenimiento oscuro y combustible para el ego (también conocido como *suministro*).

# Capítulo 3: Rasgos y comportamientos narcisistas

Puede parecer una tarea imposible, si no completamente desalentadora, predecir todos los diversos comportamientos y rasgos que mostrará un narcisista, pero una cosa para recordar es que cada uno de estos rasgos conduce a la misma causa: una autoestima debilitante. Al igual que un acosador fue una vez víctima de la intimidación a sí mismo, el comportamiento escandalosamente dañino del narcisista se debe a que otros lo trataron mal en sus años formativos, por los pensamientos en su propio cerebro, o por ambos.

**Caliente y frío.** El narcisista responde a las acciones de sus seres queridos con un arsenal de castigos. Algunos son helados, distantes, otros son explosivos y llenos de ira. Una simple cuestión como contar qué tal fue el día, puede encontrarse con un desinterés escalofriante del narcisista, interrumpido por una declaración fría como: *"No quiero escucharlo"*. Un narcisista puede intentar interrumpir la opinión impopular de un compañero. diciendo: *"Cierra la boca, ahora"*. Estas declaraciones escandalosamente groseras y combativas son cosas que el narcisista cree que tiene derecho a decir; él tiene el control porque es superior, aunque en el fondo de sí mismo, siente que es lo peor. Es el constante ping-pong de inferioridad/superioridad del que el narcisista nunca puede escapar, y todo lo que puede hacer es reaccionar, reaccionar, y reaccionar cuando otros interrumpen su sueño autoinducido de ser mejor que nadie.

Otros métodos de intimidación incluyen amenazas físicas: *"Si no lo sueltas, te daré una bofetada"* o miradas frías y heladas destinadas a disuadir a la otra persona de continuar cualquier acción o comportamiento que haya ofendido tan profundamente al narcisista.

**Giro de la realidad.** Cuando está con un narcisista, puede encontrar que las cosas van bien, la conversación transcurre sin problemas, felizmente, cuando de repente un momento después, lo acusan de algún acto terrible que nunca podría imaginar en sus sueños más salvajes. , o que algo del pasado es de repente su culpa. Es como si usted y el narcisista doblaran una esquina y el cielo se volviera negro instantáneamente y se encontrara en medio de una tormenta eléctrica. El narcisista usa esta táctica de cambio rápido para desanimarlo y confundirlo, torciendo su realidad hasta que, con el tiempo, pierde la energía para desafiar al narcisista y simplemente acepta lo que sea que dicte el narcisista como una realidad. Algunas personas pasan décadas bajo el control total de un narcisista, y si finalmente escapan, el proceso de sanación ante ellos es largo. En esencia, tienen que reconstruir sus propios sentidos, su sentido de la realidad, su propia capacidad de discernir lo que es real y lo que está fabricado.

**El narcisista es un hipócrita.** Cualquier regla que se aplique al narcisista no se aplicará a usted. Tendrá que ajustarse al presupuesto familiar y no gastar dinero en sus propios intereses o pasatiempos, pero el narcisista, por supuesto, se dará permiso para satisfacer sus pasatiempos y gustos, financieramente. El narcisista se permitirá dormir mientras usted debe estar levantado y listo para irse, o lo intimidará para que piense que debe hacer la mayor parte del trabajo de la casa, porque le resulta repugnante el desorden, una espada de doble filo, porque él también lo castigará por que la casa está desordenada, o hablará sobre qué montón de basura es la casa en general y cualquiera que viva de esta manera es un vago. Cualquiera de sus inseguridades, se convertirá en un juego justo para mantenerlo deprimido. Si alguna vez confesó que tiene problemas de autoestima debido al peso, el narcisista lo llamará gordo, si alguna vez compartió el hecho de que luchó con pensamientos suicidas en su adolescencia, el narcisista, en el fragor de una discusión, le dirá que se mate. Vivir con un narcisista es como vivir con una cobra, eventualmente, la serpiente tiene que dormir, pero todas las demás veces, su veneno es mortalmente peligroso.

**El cambio de culpa.** Por supuesto, no todos son evasivos, y no todos recibirán malos tratos quedándose acostados. El compañero que se defiende, sin embargo, está en tratamiento más extremo. Si ese compañero pierde los estribos y trata de denunciar el comportamiento abusivo del narcisista o alzar la voz, el narcisista se apresurará a señalar que el compañero es realmente enfermo mental y necesita ayuda. Tal vez en este punto, el narcisista hará otro cambio de realidad y se volverá tierno, cariñoso y le explicará a la pareja enojada cómo todo va a estar bien, solo necesitan obtener ayuda. De repente, la pareja o el ser querido que ha sufrido abusos con el tiempo, reuniendo datos como municiones, repasando momentos pasados en su cabeza para asegurarse de que tenían razón, cuestiona todas estas cosas, preguntándose si en realidad son ellos quienes están causando todos los problemas en el hogar en su lugar.

*Eres el narcisista.* Muchos han tratado de ayudar a sus compañeros narcisistas leyendo libros sobre el tema, conectándose en línea y encontrando pruebas de autoayuda para identificar rasgos narcisistas, leyendo artículos sobre narcisismo, pero si intentan llevar esta información al narcisista, podrían se culpados por exhibir rasgos de narcisismo ellos mismos. Un narcisista nunca se someterá a examen o análisis. Cada palabra que sale de su boca, es material para ser usado en su contra.

Además, cualquier deficiencia o malos hábitos o problemas mentales que usted posea siempre serán la fuente de los problemas de su relación. Si festejó demasiado en la universidad, será alcohólico. Si ganó veinte libras después del nacimiento de su hijo, será una adicta a la comida. Puede ser acusado de ser bipolar, de tener TOC, de tener un trastorno límite de la personalidad: una vez que intente llevar el análisis a la mesa, se encontrará a sí mismo como un sujeto constante de análisis por parte de un terapeuta muy sádico (y sin licencia), el narcisista mismo.

**Desinterés descarado.** Un narcisista siente cero culpa por negarse a involucrarse en algo que no le parece interesante. Si le llevara un artículo de periódico que cubriera la apertura de la galería de arte de un mejor amigo, podría mirar el periódico y luego volver a lo que estaba haciendo, sin decir nada. No siente que le deba a nadie su opinión si el tema no es digno de su interés. Los largos períodos de silencio a menudo marcan los días entre un narcisista y sus seres queridos. Él les hablará cuando lo desee, o cuando necesite algo, o cuando sea el momento de hacerles saber las formas en que le han fallado.

# Capítulo 4: Identificando rasgos narcisistas en su pareja

¿Se ha preocupado que tal vez esté en una relación con un narcisista? Es importante, tal vez incluso salvar vidas, conocer los signos antes de que se haya causado demasiado daño. Estas son algunas de las cosas a tener en cuenta y hacer preguntas. Asegúrese de comenzar a construir una red de apoyo lejos del compañero. Pueden ayudarlo a mantener un sentido de la realidad mientras navega por el terreno inestable de estar en una relación con un narcisista.

*Intratable.* Su pareja no puede aceptar que la vida sea un compromiso. Para ellos no hay compromiso: comprometerse significaría aceptar la derrota, y un narcisista nunca puede hacer eso. Es a su manera o de ninguna manera.

*Su mayor competencia.* Algunas parejas compiten de manera amistosa, especialmente cuando comparten los mismos intereses o tienen carreras similares. Tal vez corren juntos y entrenan para maratones, cada uno tratando de superar al otro en un esfuerzo por aprovechar al máximo el entrenamiento y la resistencia. Esta competencia nunca se trata de aplastar a su compañero en la derrota; sin embargo, se trata de sacar lo mejor el uno del otro a través de la competitividad amorosa. La vida con un narcisista es el espejo opuesto de esta situación ideal, tristemente. El compañero narcisista siempre intentará ser mejor en todo porque si los supera en cualquier área, lo está insultando.

*Falta de aceptación.* Una parte importante y vital de cualquier relación, ya sea entre padres e hijos, uno entre hermanos, uno entre dos amigos cercanos o entre parejas románticas, es aceptar todas las partes que crean la suma de esa persona. Algunas partes serán difíciles de vivir, algunas serán gloriosas. Algunas partes complementarán aspectos de la otra persona, pero algunas pueden chocar. La elección de seguir adelante con otra persona en la sociedad es el acto de amor. Desafortunadamente, un narcisista no puede amar. Ella está cableada incorrectamente para la emoción. Nunca será aceptado por ella, ni lo bueno, ni lo malo o lo feo. Simplemente está ahí para distraerla del vacío dentro de sí misma.

*Usted hace las cosas peor.* La vida puede estar llena de momentos estresantes: enfermedades, problemas en el trabajo, facturas, problemas para criar hijos. Con un compañero narcisista, todas estas cosas empeorarán con su presencia, sus acciones y su aporte. Nada de lo que haga será suficiente y, de hecho, lo que haga y diga puede ser atribuido a la causa de muchos de estos problemas.

*Hipercrítica.* ¿Alguna vez ha tenido un amigo al que le encantaba asistir a funciones sociales solo para golpear a las otras personas en la fiesta? Tal vez tuvo un asiento en primera fila viendo estas situaciones, riendo y sacudiendo su cabeza ante cada cosa escandalosa y mordaz que esa persona tenía que decir sobre los demás, burlándose de su ropa, su apariencia, su elección de pareja o carrera. Es posible que se haya sentido culpable por no mencionarle nada a la persona por su comportamiento grosero, pero fue muy gracioso en ese momento. Ahora, desafortunadamente, está conectado con alguien, el narcisista, que le pone a usted ese ojo mordaz y a todos los demás en su vida, y no tiene nada de gracioso. La proximidad a ese foco de críticas candente puede sentirse, con el tiempo, como si estuviera viviendo al lado de un reactor nuclear.

*¿Dónde está la empatía?* Cuando se toma un momento y mira detenidamente a la persona que cree que puede ser narcisista, ¿ve empatía? Cuando intenta explicarle cómo se siente respecto a algo, ¿ha visto un destello de comprensión o desinterés? ¿Ha habido alguna vez un momento en el que realmente creía que esa persona se ponía en los zapatos de otra persona? Si no, es muy probable que sean narcisistas o tengan tendencias narcisistas.

*¿Se ha preguntado más de una vez si esta persona le ama?* Es posible que haya escuchado las palabras pronunciadas, pero ¿las ha creído?

*Salir con los niños.* Esta es una pregunta difícil porque seamos honestos, no todos disfrutan de la compañía de los niños. Pero incluso la persona más retraída les dará a los niños una parte de su tiempo, especialmente si están saliendo o viviendo con los padres de un niño. Y aunque no digan mucho o particularmente disfruten de estar presentes en reuniones de té con su hija, instintivamente saben que estar presente, a veces, es lo correcto. Sin embargo, un narcisista no tendrá parte, incluso encerrándose en una habitación para mantenerse alejado de los niños.

Sobre el tema de los niños, si tiene niños, observe cómo reaccionan con su pareja. ¿Parece que siempre están tratando de ganarse el afecto o la atención de ellos? O si ha estado en esta relación durante un período de tiempo más prolongado, ¿nota que los niños se quedan callados con su pareja, posiblemente con miedo de compartir algo con ellos por miedo al rechazo o las críticas? Si sus hijos parecen incómodos, especialmente si la relación ha durado más de unos pocos meses, eso podría ser una gran señal de alerta de que algo no está bien.

***Las opiniones de otros sobre su pareja no coinciden.*** Muchos de nosotros hemos salido con alguien que es un bicho raro. Tal vez vemos lo bueno en ellos donde otros no. Pero si sus amigos, parientes, incluso conocidos siguen diciéndole que tuvieron una *"mala vibra"* o notaron un comportamiento particularmente negativo: *"Fui a estrecharle la mano y ella simplemente me miró, luego se alejó",* tal vez debería escuchar con más atención a sus propios instintos, también.

***Mintiendo.*** Este es quizás el aspecto más difícil de abordar porque tiene que encontrar la fuerza, para ser honesto consigo mismo. Tal vez su realidad ya esté en terreno inestable. Tal vez ya ha comenzado a cuestionar sus propios poderes de observación. Si puede recordar los momentos en que su pareja audazmente, obviamente mintió, y luego trató con todas sus fuerzas para convencerlo de lo contrario, debe buscar ayuda de inmediato. Este es uno de los mayores signos de que está enredado con un narcisista.

Una cosa que puede ayudarlo a mantener un control firme sobre la realidad es escribir cosas o incluso grabar conversaciones. Ahora que los teléfonos celulares tienen la capacidad de grabar, puede ser mucho más fácil hacerlo sutilmente sin que el narcisista potencial se dé cuenta de que lo está grabando. Intente que no lo atrapen. Incluso si tuviera que repetirle las palabras del narcisista, el enfoque siempre estaría en la traición del acto de grabar la conversación, no en la conversación misma.

# Capítulo 5: Relaciones tóxicas vs. saludables

## Fuerte sentido del yo

No es necesario estar involucrado con un narcisista para experimentar el amor tóxico, pero es útil tener una base sólida y conocimiento de lo que está relacionado con una relación tóxica y qué es lo que la hace verdaderamente saludable.

Muchas personas creen que el compañero ideal los "complementará", por lo que buscan a alguien como si estuvieran buscando un pedazo perdido de sí mismos. Este tipo de pensamiento realmente puede hacerlo el blanco perfecto para un narcisista. Su objetivo a lo largo de la vida debe ser crecer como una persona completa: el compañero ideal no lo complementará porque ya es 100% usted, pero lo halagarán.

Hay dos lados de la moneda cuando se trata de una relación: uno puede continuar buscando el crecimiento personal y el aprendizaje con el apoyo y el aliento de su pareja (y esto debería ir en ambos sentidos), o alguno puede estar obsesionado con la relación en sí. Este último no es saludable y conduce a la codependencia, y tener una mentalidad como esta, nuevamente lo convierte en una víctima potencial de un narcisista.

## Estancamiento

Si no crece, ¿realmente está viviendo su mejor vida? Muchas parejas temerán el crecimiento y el cambio en sus parejas porque significa que la relación también cambiará. Sin embargo, el cambio es parte de la vida e indica una relación saludable, pero no cuando solo una pareja está cambiando. El amor saludable alienta a cada compañero a ser fiel a sí mismo y a su propio camino. El amor tóxico tiene parejas que intentan permanecer igual, como gemelos, para que nadie se sienta abandonado. Esta tendencia de inseguridad proviene de la necesidad de una prueba de amor. Por el contrario, una prueba de amor saludable es la voluntad de apoyar a la pareja a medida que cambian y evolucionan naturalmente.

### Individuales pero juntos

Una relación sana es aquella en la que ambos compañeros se sienten seguros persiguiendo sus propios intereses y amistades fuera de la relación. El amor por los deportes o las artes, el aire libre o las actividades personales no son cosas que amenacen la base de la relación, sino que la fortalecen, ya que cada pareja tiene experiencias únicas que puede llevar a casa para compartir con su pareja amorosa y solidaria. Una relación tóxica, por otro lado, es aquella en la que los compañeros se aíslan del mundo exterior, volviéndose más solitarios y miopes, a menudo cortando lazos con familiares o amigos mientras hibernan en un mundo claustrofóbico en el que el crecimiento es imposible.

Además, una relación saludable es aquella en la que el papel del liderazgo depende de la dinámica de cada individuo. A veces, un compañero se siente más cómodo con el otro compañero que toma la mayoría de las decisiones financieras. Otras veces, toman grandes decisiones juntos pero intercambian roles cuando deben decidirse asuntos más pequeños. Cualquiera que sea la dinámica particular, se basa en el amor y la confianza, no en el poder o el control. Una relación saludable es aquella en la que cada individuo puede ver sus propias fortalezas y debilidades y sabe que puede confiar en que su pareja sea fuerte en áreas donde no lo son, y la vergüenza no juega ningún papel en reconocer esto.

**Amar lo que ya es cierto**

Muchas personas hablan de cómo un compañero potencial sería una buen "partido", pero que primero cambiarían algunas cosas. Los seres humanos no deben ser moldeados o entrenados para adaptarse al ideal de otra persona. Ese tipo de amor nunca dará como resultado una relación saludable. En una relación sana, cada pareja se ama por lo que ya son, lo que eran antes de que comenzara la relación y lo que se están convirtiendo cada día que pasa. Eso no quiere decir que las conductas problemáticas o los períodos de la vida, como la adicción, la depresión, los problemas en el trabajo o los cambios profesionales importantes, el duelo por la pérdida de un ser querido o una lesión o enfermedad no proporcionen contratiempos y desafíos a la relación. Sin embargo, si ambos compañeros aprecian quién son de forma honesta, pueden superar estos desafíos con una mayor probabilidad de éxito.

Si usted o su pareja creen que pueden *"arreglarse"* o *"entrenarse"* mutuamente, estos son signos de pensamiento tóxico, y demuestran que, la persona que cree que puede lograr estas cosas con una pareja, aún no está lista para una relación saludable.

**Desapego**

El desapego es un tema aterrador para muchas personas. Aquellos que sufren del trastorno límite de la personalidad pueden encontrar este concepto particularmente desafiante cuando todavía están lidiando con sentimientos de abandono. Sin embargo, el desprendimiento es necesario para evitar el estancamiento y la codependencia. ¿Se imagina que no puede funcionar correctamente si un cónyuge o pareja se va de viaje de negocios de dos semanas? En una relación saludable, tal ausencia podría ser un desafío, y la soledad ciertamente podría entrar en juego, pero la pareja en casa aún podría ir a trabajar, ducharse, comer comidas saludables y practicar el cuidado personal. En una relación codependiente, la pareja en el hogar podría encontrarse tan incapacitada por los sentimientos de abandono y paranoia que podría hacer poco más que quedarse acostada en la cama, torturada por la preocupación y los pensamientos negativos.

La codependencia conduce a la obsesión, y la obsesión resulta en un colapso de sí mismo: autoestima, cuidado personal. El narcisista inconscientemente quiere un compañero así. Son perfectamente adecuados para ser moldeados y manipulados para los ejercicios y caprichos diarios del narcisista.

## Gratificación y derecho

El sexo a menudo se usa como una herramienta entre parejas. Puede ser utilizado como una recompensa, o como un medio para ganar afirmación. Me *siento atractiva y sexy porque tuvo relaciones sexuales conmigo*, o sé que ella no me dejará mientras tengamos relaciones sexuales de manera regular. Estos pactos tácitos realizados entre la pareja codependiente hacen lo contrario de fortalecer la relación; lo dividen en una serie de maniobras y juegos de poder.

Buscar una gratificación inmediata a expensas de la pareja no es de lo que se trata una relación saludable. Cada compañero no está allí para servir al otro. Cada día es una opción para avanzar en amor con respeto y desprendimiento amoroso.

**El poder de estar solo**

Muchas personas no pueden soportar momentos de soledad. En cambio, buscan a su pareja en todo momento para evitar sentimientos abrumadores de soledad. Sin embargo, una persona sana puede encontrar paz y sanación en momentos de aislamiento. En lugar de miedo, hay momentos de claridad y conciencia. En lugar de pánico, hay paz. Una relación sana tiene espacio para que cada pareja siga su propio camino de vez en cuando, y estas parejas encuentran que después, la reunión es mucho más dulce.

# Capítulo 6: Narcisismo en las relaciones

**Algunos narcisistas son buscadores de curiosidad,** objetivan y enfocan a alguien por una multitud de razones que se centran en las cualidades únicas, el patrimonio o las opciones de vida de la futura pareja. Quizás estas cualidades tienen que ver con la raza o la cultura o con una gran diferencia de edad. Quizás tengan una elección de carrera o un pasatiempo inusual. Cualquiera que sea la razón, el narcisista puede pasar rápidamente de ser un admirador a ser un liberador de desprecio odioso y prejuicioso. Estas relaciones pueden ser particularmente dolorosas y devastadoras para la pareja del narcisista, ya que trabajan para derribar y menospreciar las mismas cosas que hacen de esta pareja quienes son. Ser odiado por aspectos vitales de usted mismo es algo que nadie debería tener que soportar.

Los narcisistas **centrados** en el odio están buscando un compañero en el crimen, al principio. Al igual que ese desprecio de la fiesta que vio en primera fila de los comentarios hilarantes y de espíritu cruel sobre otros asistentes, este narciso navega por la vida, un crítico de todos los demás que están a su lado. Al principio, eres la mano derecha de este narcisista porque eres "mejor", eres "especial", pero no pasará mucho tiempo antes de que usted se una a la refriega de aquellos que el narcisista considera dignos de ridículo.

## Enamorarse de un narcisista

Los estudios muestran que los primeros siete encuentros que tiene con un narcisista lo dejarán impresionado con lo positivos, educados y encantadores que son. La clave para entender en lo que se está metiendo es enfocarse en el hecho de que un narcisista simplemente no puede mantener su fachada social o emocional: no es real, se practica a partir de años de observar cómo se comportan otras personas, tal vez personas que el narcisista alguna vez envidió. En una situación social, muchos narcisistas brillan absolutamente, encantando a todos en la fiesta o cena con su sensibilidad y adulación. Sin embargo, una vez que finaliza el evento, solo el compañero del narcisista puede ver cómo se siente realmente el narcisista y puede escuchar todo sobre los diversos invitados al evento y todas sus fallas. Lo mismo puede decirse de la propia pareja. Una vez que termine el período de luna de miel de la relación, escucharán todo sobre sus propias fallas, todos los días y varias veces al día.

Al igual que el animal terrestre más rápido del mundo, el guepardo no puede mantener sus impresionantes velocidades más allá de un corto período de tiempo, por lo que el narcisista eventualmente debe soltar ese encanto increíble para revelar su verdadera identidad.

El compañero de un narcisista tiene asientos de primera fila para todo tipo de comportamiento terrible. Verán al narcisista ser grosero de esperar en un restaurante, o coquetear lascivamente con alguien en una fiesta justo en frente de ellos. Verán que el narcisista se niega a ceder su asiento en un tren a una persona mayor o corta la cabeza de una línea de boletos, sin pensar en absoluto en las quejas de los otros que estuvieron allí primero. La burbuja narcisista gira solo en torno a ellos mismos y el resto del mundo simplemente no existe.

Un narcisista mantendrá todos sus mejores rasgos bajo un microscopio y los diseccionará. Para un narcisista, la arrogancia es sexy y la amabilidad es lamentable porque el hecho de tratar bien a alguien además de sí mismo es un signo de debilidad integral. Lo reprenderán por ayudar a una persona necesitada cuando, en cambio, podría haber estado avivando las llamas de su propio ego. Lo derribarán una y otra vez solo por ser usted mismo, y si es una persona cariñosa, con el tiempo comenzará a creer que usted es el monstruo, cuando ha sido el narcisista todo el tiempo.

Algunas personas pueden volverse adictas a estar enamoradas de los narcisistas, estrictamente por la intensidad del comienzo de la relación y particularmente aquellos que han sido criados en hogares tóxicos y han desarrollado hábitos de codependencia. Estas personas pobres han cambiado el verdadero amor por una producción más brillante que la vida. Están enganchados a la intensidad del romance, el sexo, la adoración constante, antes de la inevitable caída en la oscuridad.

Una forma de convencer a un narcisista para que revele su verdadera naturaleza es ser ingenuo cuando está en su presencia. Si bien un narcisista podría pretender adorar la confianza durante la etapa de cortejo de su relación, de hecho, reaccionará negativamente a cualquiera que parezca mejor de lo que es. Si se rebaja a ellos, obtendrán el exceso de confianza necesario para comenzar a confiar en usted mucho más de lo que confiarían en nadie más. Incluso puede lograr que revelen lo poco que piensan del resto del mundo, y esa es una gran señal de alerta de que son narcisistas, incluso las personas más odiosas tienen al menos una persona que les gusta o admiran; el narcisista no tiene ninguno.

**Nunca use la palabra "narcisista".** Dese cuenta de que un narcisista se odia más a sí mismo y carece por completo del valor o la fortaleza para enfrentarse a lo que es. El uso de términos psicológicos no solo desencadenará la ira narcisista en el narcisista, sino que sus palabras inevitablemente se convertirán en armas verbales contra usted. Si está investigando el narcisismo para comprender mejor su relación con uno, por todos los medios, mantenga su investigación en secreto. O bien, dentro de unos días o semanas, descubrirá que usted es el etiquetado como narcisista.

# Capítulo 7: Los diferentes tipos de narcisistas

## Un espectro de narcisismo

La medicina y la psicología modernas están llegando a comprender, cada vez más, que el cerebro humano es demasiado complejo para ser encasillado en una sola categoría, ya sea con respecto a aquellos en el espectro del autismo, aquellos con desafíos de déficit de atención o aquellos con desafíos únicos como problemas de aprendizaje como dislexia o incluso daltonismo. Todo esto, por supuesto, no inhibe a una persona de llevar una vida feliz y plena. De hecho, algunos como el espectro del autismo permiten a la persona ver la vida desde un punto de vista único, uno que para ciertas personas puede ser un impulso en áreas creativas o incluso en entornos terapéuticos.

El espectro del narcisismo, sin embargo, es una categoría muy diferente.

## Narcisistas clásicos

Estos narcisistas abarcan desde una persona adicta al trabajo hambrienta de poder hasta una exhibicionista. Suelen tener mucho éxito en la vida pero no tienen relaciones saludables. La única forma en que pueden sentirse bien consigo mismos es si están en el centro de atención, mostrando sus logros y asegurándose de que nadie desafíe su lugar en el pedestal de la vida.

## Narcisistas frágiles o quebradizos

Estas son personas encerradas, que en el fondo creen que realmente son mejores que los demás, pero desprecian ser el centro de atención. Pueden ser de naturaleza parásita, sombreando a aquellos cuya atención o logros desean ser suyos.

# Narcisistas extremos o "malignos"

### El narcisista basado en el conocimiento.

Este tipo de narcisista puede ser manejado correctamente, prácticamente inofensivo. Tienden a haber adquirido una gran cantidad de conocimiento en diversas áreas específicas y pueden ser ávidos coleccionistas de curiosidades. Disfrutan escuchándose hablar y no tienen ningún interés en la opinión o comentarios que usted tenga sobre el tema sobre el que están pontificando. Mientras usted finja escuchar, no recibirá ningún desafío directo de este tipo de narcisista, simplemente no entre en un debate con ellos.

### El narcisista basado en logros

Este narcisista puede ser bastante encantador, y es posible que admire sus diversos logros (que es parte de lo que atrae a las personas a su web). Puede ser extremadamente ambicioso y es muy posible que haya verdaderos puntos de orgullo junto con su jactancia. Puede que en la primera reunión piense que esta es una persona excelente para establecer contactos, pero tenga en cuenta que usted solo está en el planeta para servirle, y no al revés. En el momento en que ya no esté en él por él, él lo descartará.

### El narcisista basado en la seducción

Este narcisista se concentra en cualquier sensación de necesidad o baja autoestima, e inunda a esa persona con halagos, elogios e incluso coqueteo. Este narcisista hará que parezca que lo ha puesto a usted en un pedestal y haría cualquier cosa para ser como usted, pero esto es, por supuesto, una artimaña. Inevitablemente cambiará las tornas y su objetivo es que usted sea su admirador y no al revés.

## El narcisista cruel

Este narcisista saca sus patadas del sadismo. Para sentirse como si fuera mejor que los demás, utilizará comentarios crueles, dosis abundantes de sarcasmo e incluso bromas prácticas para hacer que su objetivo sea el hazmerreír de la oficina o la familia. Expresará sus necesidades amenazándolo. Es lo contrario de encantador. Si trabaja con alguien así, la mejor manera de lidiar con él es actuar completamente neutral, manteniendo la firme creencia en usted mismo y que no merece un trato abusivo. Cualquier desafío directo solo aumentará las cosas y no a su favor.

## El narcisista basado en la venganza

Este narcisista puede guardar rencor durante mucho tiempo, posiblemente para siempre. Si alguna vez estuvo casado con esta persona, es posible que haya intentado poner a sus hijos o familiares en su contra. Jugarán a la víctima para hacerle parecer un monstruo. Si usted se cruzó en el trabajo, el narcisista basado en la venganza intentará hacerle perder el ascenso, ser despedido o incluso ser acusado de acoso sexual. Su ego es tan frágil y su venganza tan grande, que sus vidas giran completamente en torno a complots para hacer que sus víctimas sean completamente miserables.

Si se ha cruzado con este narcisista muy peligroso, mantenga un rastro de evidencia o correos electrónicos en papel, cualquier cosa que pueda demostrar a los demás de qué cosas verdaderamente malvadas se han hecho. Es posible que deba obtener una orden de restricción contra ellos.

# Encubierto vs. Abierto, Cerebral vs. Somático

La regla general aquí es que los narcisistas clásicos serán abiertos en sus comportamientos y los narcisistas frágiles siempre tomarán la ruta encubierta. Los narcisistas extremos emplearán ambos tipos de tácticas para obtener lo que quieren y necesitan.

El subtipo del narcisista cerebral hace que se centren principalmente en lo que saben. Les preocupa poco la apariencia física y tienden a despreciar a quienes se preocupan por cosas tan superficiales. El narcisista somático, sin embargo, estará obsesionado con un poco más. Perseguirán eternamente la juventud, ya sea mediante una cirugía plástica o probando dietas interminables o siguiendo un estricto régimen de ejercicios sin perder un día. Juzgarán a otros que están menos preocupados por la apariencia con bastante dureza.

Lo que todos los narcisistas tienen en común es la sensación de nunca ser completamente apreciado o entendido. Viven sus vidas en un estado constante de desear que alguien finalmente pueda ver cuán estupendos son. Un narcisista a menudo se siente como una víctima. Culpará a todos los demás por sus errores menos a sí mismo.

Muchos narcisistas no lo pensarán dos veces antes de engañar a sus clientes o robar de la compañía para la que trabajan. Cualquier medio que deban tomar para cumplir sus objetivos, lo toman. Los narcisistas no son dadores, todo lo que dan tiene una cuerda atada. Son maestros de la ilusión y se necesita un buen oído atento y un ojo vigilante para detectarlos en un mar de humanidad imperfecta.

Finalmente, un nuevo subtipo de narcisismo se llama narcisista basado en la comunidad. A menudo verá a esta persona en las redes sociales porque, en esta era moderna, ese es el mejor foro para ella. Constantemente compartirá sobre el bien que está haciendo en el mundo, cuán activa es y cuán perfecta es su apariencia como lo demuestran las fotografías bien organizadas. Pensará que es mejor que nadie debido a todas las tareas que realiza y la cantidad de tiempo que dona a otros, y su ego depende de la cantidad de me gusta, acciones o comentarios que gana en las publicaciones de sus cuentas de redes sociales.

# Capítulo 8: Narcisismo en familias

Crecer en una estructura familiar narcisista puede ser similar a vivir en una casa embrujada. Uno puede sentir que algo anda mal pero nunca ver la verdad desde las sombras. Los niños que crecen con narcisismo sienten una sensación subyacente de ira y fatalidad todo el tiempo. Sin embargo, aprenden a no llamar la atención sobre sus miedos, porque hacer esas preguntas se considera lo mismo que criticar, y un padre narcisista nunca debe sentir que está siendo criticado.

Es posible que los niños que crecen con ellos nunca entiendan completamente el conjunto de reglas tácitas que un padre o padres narcisistas imponen en sus hijos (algunos narcisistas solo se enamoran de otros narcisistas), pero los niños aprenden a obedecer esas reglas al pie de la letra. Los niños que sobreviven a un hogar narcisista a menudo hablan de ira y abandono intensos y sin explotar, dolor profundamente arraigado y una sensación de traición, pero no pueden señalar con el dedo la causa de ninguno de estos sentimientos. Solo saben que siempre los han tenido. Muchas veces, incluso se culpan por ellos y por no ser lo suficientemente buenos o dignos de respeto o amor.

Los hijos de los narcisistas tienen que guardar un secreto del resto del mundo, incluso, tal vez sus amigos más cercanos o familiares. Los secretos que pueden tener que guardar es que no se les está cuidando realmente emocionalmente y que, posiblemente, se está abusando de ellos de alguna manera. Aprenden a poner siempre la sonrisa perfecta en su rostro para ocultar la verdad.

Los niños también pueden ser alimentados con la creencia tóxica de que ellos y el resto de la familia son mejores que los demás: mejor que los vecinos, mejor que las familias de sus amigos, mejor que los otros niños en la escuela, mejor incluso que el resto de la familia. Al mismo tiempo, estos niños pueden estar recibiendo el mensaje hablado (o no hablado) de que ellos mismos no son lo suficientemente buenos, físicamente bonitos o guapos, no son lo suficientemente inteligentes, no son lo suficientemente capaces, porque para un narcisista, los niños son a la vez competencia y sirvientes del narcisista.

**Una familia atrasada.** En una familia narcisista, los padres no cuidan a los niños, el cuidado de los niños están basados en una serie de mandatos, que muestren un apoyo inquebrantable, un sinfín de muestras de amor y afecto, y posiblemente incluso tareas domésticas por encima y más allá de lo que un niño normal debería hacer, ya que realizar tareas serviles puede quitarle tiempo al narcisista para perseguir sus propios objetivos.

**Triangulación.** Esta es una forma de comunicación particularmente cruel, donde un miembro de la familia envía información o un mensaje a otro miembro de la familia no directamente, sino a través de un tercer miembro de la familia. *"Dile a tu padre que es un pedazo de basura". "Dile a tu hermana que si sigue comiendo así, la gente la llamará gorda".*

Cuando un narcisista elude esta forma de comunicación pasivo-agresiva, es porque está furioso: la comunicación directa a menudo solo se reserva para ocasiones especiales, como cuando uno de los hijos o el cónyuge de un narcisista rechaza su trato por el narcisista, o dice o hace algo que el narcisista cree que es un ataque directo.

# Capítulo 9: Lista de verificación de abuso

Debido a que estar conectado con un narcisista desgasta lentamente sus poderes de percepción, puede ser difícil dar un paso atrás y determinar si, de hecho, es víctima de abuso. Esta lista lo ayudará a reconocer cualquier síntoma o reacción que sea una señal de abuso a manos de un narcisista.

**Se enferma más a menudo y se siente deteriorado.** El abuso emocional y psicológico no es solo un asalto constante al cerebro sino también al cuerpo. El estrés y la angustia desencadenan la liberación de la hormona cortisol, que a su vez promueve fatiga, aumento o pérdida de peso, depresión y sentimientos de desesperanza. El exceso de cortisol en el cuerpo puede desencadenar el envejecimiento prematuro. Además, el estrés constante durante todo el día puede afectar negativamente el ciclo de sueño. Si descubre que tiene alguno de estos síntomas, podría deberse a una relación tóxica.

**Le falta la confianza que solía tener.**

De hecho, descubre que está caminando sobre cáscaras de huevo todo el tiempo. En lugar de compartir inmediatamente una noticia, un acontecimiento de su día, un pensamiento creativo o una broma divertida que escuchó, se censura a sí mismo, se calla por miedo a que lo excluyan, critiquen o castiguen por un desaire leve.

Sus límites pueden haber desaparecido también. Donde una vez tenía líneas distintas que prefería no cruzar, ahora simplemente se dibujan en la arena y su compañero camina sobre ellas.

Estos nuevos hábitos ahora pueden extenderse más allá de su relación. Es posible que también sea más complaciente en el trabajo, con menos ambición, impulso y voz para hablar cuando su jefe o compañeros de trabajo lo empujan o pasan por alto sus esfuerzos.

**Sus deseos y necesidades básicas parecen haberse desvanecido.** Digamos que su rutina matutina solía ser preparar café, leer el periódico o las noticias en su teléfono, salir a caminar o correr con el perro antes de bañarse y vestirse para el trabajo. Ahora, sin embargo, se levanta temprano para preparar un desayuno completo y servir a su pareja en la cama. Tal vez tenga que correr a la tienda por algo menor que su compañero haya encontrado de vital importancia en el último minuto. Ha comenzado a llegar tarde al trabajo o a la escuela cuando siempre era puntual antes. Llega a la oficina y descubre que ni siquiera ha desayunado o tomado café, y no puede recordar la última vez que se tomó un tiempo para hacer ejercicio.

Las partes de usted que son de "usted" simplemente están desapareciendo ante sus ojos. No hay más usted, solo hay un ayudante, sirviente o asistente personal para su compañero, y sus días y noches pasan volando, totalmente consumidos por las tareas que su compañero establece ante usted.

**La vida se ha convertido en una serie de emergencias y averías.** Usted y su pareja planearon un viaje a una ciudad cercana para visitar los centros comerciales y restaurantes. Usted reservó una reserva en un hotel, y el viaje a la ciudad fue agradable. Pasó varias paradas de descanso y se detuvo en una para ir al baño, pero su pareja nunca mencionó que tenían hambre ni le pidieron que dejara de comer.

Ahora está en la habitación del hotel y su compañero está en silencio. Sabe que algo malo está por suceder. Cuando le pregunta qué quiere comer su pareja para cenar, obtiene más silencio. Han pasado dos horas e incluso siente que se muere de hambre. Su pareja comienza a llorar o se encierra en el baño, o enciende la televisión y le ignora por completo. Si pregunta "¿qué está pasando?", Es posible que escuche una respuesta como *Sabes lo que está pasando"*. Sus mini vacaciones perfectas se han convertido en otra pesadilla.

Nunca se sabe cuándo ocurrirá la próxima emergencia, solo el narcisista lo sabe. No importa qué tan atento intente ser, qué tan bien trate de planificar, algo va a salir mal, y cuando lo haga, será su culpa.

A veces solo usted será el objetivo. Tal vez necesitaba que su pareja hiciera algo de vital importancia, como dejar el papeleo en un día en que no podía salir de la oficina o recoger a su hijo de la escuela cuando la enfermera llamó y le dijo que estaba enfermo. El narcisista utilizará estos momentos como oportunidades perfectas para sacudir su mundo y no en el buen sentido. Quieren verlo devastado tan a menudo como sea posible, especialmente si ha estado tratando de mantenerse fuera del agua a raíz de sus ataques.

**Hipervigilancia.** Esta reacción también continúa mucho después de que la víctima haya logrado abandonar su Abuso Narcisista. Escucha constantemente que el auto de su pareja se detiene en el camino de entrada o anda de puntillas por el apartamento tratando de no despertar a su pareja por la mañana. Mantiene una oreja en cualquier habitación en la que esté su pareja, especialmente si tiene hijos y ellos están en la misma habitación. Escucha los cambios en el tono de voz de su compañero que podrían indicar la próxima pelea. O usted revisa su propio teléfono y su correo electrónico constantemente para ver si recibió un mensaje encriptado de su pareja; esto sucederá incluso después de que lo haya dejado, porque a los narcisistas les gusta regresar para recuperar a sus ex cuando no tienen suficiente suministro en sus vidas.

**Está pensando en hacerse daño.** Quizás haya comenzado en secreto una cuenta regresiva para el día en que terminará su vida. O tal vez a altas horas de la noche, cuando su pareja está dormida, se queda en el baño detrás de una puerta cerrada, haciéndose daño. Tal vez conduce al trabajo e imagina conducir a la autopista. Todo esto lo aterrorizan, pero los pensamientos siguen llegando. No ve una salida.

**Se está apartando de todos los demás excepto de su pareja.** Tal vez se avergüence de la situación en la que se ha metido, así que dejó de compartir con sus amigos lo que está sucediendo en su vida. Su pareja le ha hecho demasiado lío por salir sin ella, pero nunca quiere salir en pareja, o nunca quiere salir con usted y sus amigos, o cuando sale en grupo, su pareja es tan grosera con sus amigos que desearía nunca haber salido en primer lugar. Entonces, se queda en casa noche tras noche, perdiéndose en el vórtice que es la dinámica sofocante entre usted y la pareja que dirige su vida.

**Auto-sabotaje.** No solo es más pasivo y temeroso en el lugar de trabajo, sino que en todos los aspectos de la vida, ha dejado de ser un emprendedor. Los proyectos que comenzó con gusto están acumulando polvo. Las rutinas que comenzó a mejorar usted mismo: entrenar, ir a terapia, yoga, jardinería, se están quedando en el camino a medida que se siente menos seguro, más agotado, más confundido día a día en cuanto a la dirección que debe ir. Es posible que esté dejando pasar los plazos, convencido de que no tenía posibilidades de éxito independientemente de sus esperanzas y sueños iniciales.

**Disociación.** Se encuentra "desconectado" en momentos de estrés extremo y descubre que ha perdido tiempo o no puede recordar los detalles exactos de una situación.

**Empieza a preguntarse si usted es el abusivo.** Este es quizás el efecto más insidioso que un narcisista tiene en su pareja, realmente convincente, con el tiempo y a través de métodos como la proyección, hacer luz de gas, la redirección y el enfriamiento, usted cree que usted es la persona narcisista o mentalmente enferma. Empieza a cuestionar cada movimiento y palabra, preguntándose si, de hecho, tiene alguna empatía. Quizás usted solo se importa a sí mismo. Pero si es así, ¿por qué estaría aquí sirviendo a su pareja? Es posible que su pareja ya haya tratado de convencerlo de que, de hecho, no los está sirviendo, sino que los está torturando, manteniéndolos presionados. Esta devastadora destrucción de sí mismo es a menudo lo que mantiene a las víctimas con sus parejas abusivas durante años, décadas o de por vida.

La verdad es que debe tener el coraje de descubrir que ninguna parte de este abuso ha sido su culpa. Nada de eso. La fuerza para darse cuenta de eso y continuar con la recuperación es enorme, pero si ha sobrevivido hasta aquí, es lo suficientemente fuerte como para sobrevivir al escape, y lo suficientemente fuerte como para que algún día comience a sanar.

# Capítulo 10: Cómo tomar el control de su vida

Lo más difícil de recuperarse de Abuso Narcisista es el distanciamiento real del narcisista. Su compañero narcisista moverá el cielo y la Tierra para tratar de evitar que se vaya, de todas las maneras desagradables que pueda imaginar, incluidas amenazas, calumnias, destrucción de propiedades y complicadas batallas legales. A veces, puede parecer más fácil simplemente rendirse y quedarse con su abusador, pero no debe rendirse: un futuro más feliz es posible, incluso si el camino por delante va a ser accidentado.

**Llegar a un acuerdo con un sistema de creencias destrozado.** Hay muchas cosas por las que tendrá que trabajar y aceptar después de darse cuenta de que su pareja es un narcisista y decidir trabajar para lograr la independencia de la relación. Primero, tendrá que procesar eso donde antes creía en la bondad de la humanidad, ahora está cuestionando esa creencia, preguntándose cómo puede volver a confiar en alguien después de ver cómo se ve el verdadero mal.

Además, avanzará sin un solo recuerdo feliz para conservar el valor sentimental. Todo momento del pasado de esta relación será doloroso de recordar. Eso no es fácil, porque incluso en las relaciones difíciles, generalmente hay buenos momentos para aferrarse y decir: *"bueno, al menos lo intentamos".* Tanto usted como el narcisista intentaron, pero para diferentes fines: el narcisista intentó mantenerlo abajo, y simplemente usted trató de sobrevivir.

**Pasos a seguir antes de que pueda comenzar la recuperación.** Antes de que esté listo para que comience la sanación, tendrá que adquirir la mentalidad para avanzar hacia el proceso de sanación en sí. Esa mentalidad incluye algunas lecciones muy dolorosas, incluidas la comprensión y la aceptación de que nada sobre su relación con el narcisista era lo que parecía. Esto puede ser algo devastador de aceptar. Es posible que se sienta conmocionado hasta el fondo, por usar el término que comúnmente usan los veteranos que padecen TEPT. Los episodios diarios y nocturnos de abusos sin sentido, constantes y devastadores y la ira reaccionaria, pueden nivelar a la persona más fuerte.

Una vez que se da cuenta de que todo fue una mentira, la siguiente etapa de recuperación puede ser aún más agotadora. Comenzará a ver, ya sea solo, en retrospectiva y autorrealización, o con la ayuda de un terapeuta, todas las señales de alerta que omitió o ignoró al entrar, y durante el resto de la relación. En este punto, puede comenzar a dudar de su propia inteligencia o agudeza, pero no debería. Culpar a la víctima está mal, incluso cuando, o *especialmente cuando*, la víctima es usted mismo.

Después de que los sentimientos de pena por la pérdida de su propio poder hayan disminuido un poco, puede comenzar a sentir enojo, incluso ira, por ser ridiculizado. Puede descubrir que está enojado consigo mismo por participar en su propia destrucción a través de los diseños del narcisista. Es probable que reflexionar, repasar los eventos pasados y encontrar los aspectos negativos en ellos, es lo que sucederá ahora, una y otra vez, y revivir esos oscuros momentos emocionales puede ser difícil de hacer por sí mismo. Un terapeuta es el mejor para ayudarlo a  sortear estas tormentas internas que son necesarias para que usted pueda enfrentarlas y avanzar hacia la sanación.

Trate de evitar tener diálogos internos como *"Solo un idiota caería en eso"* o *"Debe haber algo malo conmigo que permití que esto sucediera"*. Si bien es comprensible que piense estas cosas sobre usted mismo, no hay nada útil sobre estos pensamientos y le impedirán cualquier tipo de sanación y recuperación.

Por otro lado, es perfectamente saludable y está dentro de su derecho, examinar sus acciones y decisiones pasadas y darse cuenta de los errores que ha cometido, como quedarse cuando consideró irse o perdonar las acciones y palabras abusivas de su pareja narcisista. Al reconocer estos errores, puede evitar volver a cometerlos en el futuro. Debe decirse a sí mismo *"nunca más"*.

## Aprendiendo a ser poderoso otra vez

Durante un tiempo, tal vez incluso mucho tiempo, después de dejar una relación tóxica con un narcisista, puede continuar su día en piloto automático, completar tareas y hacer cosas, pero nunca tomar decisiones, nunca avanzar con ningún sentido de propósito. Eso es porque ha pasado tanto tiempo sin su poder; nadie en una posición constante de defensa es capaz de ser proactivo sobre las cosas. Una vez que se da cuenta de que ahora está caminando por la vida, como un robot, puede comenzar a tomar medidas para recuperar su fuerza y propósito anteriores. Haga una lista de cosas pequeñas y fáciles que le gustaría lograr en una semana o en un mes. Vaya a su propio ritmo. No sienta culpa por el tiempo que le lleve. Está en entrenamiento ahora, o más bien, rehabilitación. Estás re-aprendiendo cómo ser un ser humano decidido, vital y fuerte.

En este momento, es su propia fuerza de voluntad la que lo llevará a través de la oscuridad hacia el otro lado, hacia la felicidad nuevamente. Es lo único que tiene, aparte de amigos y familiares y un terapeuta. Desafortunadamente, incluso las personas más comprensivas, no pueden estar dentro de su propia cabeza, protegiéndose de las palabras falsas e hirientes que el narcisista ha dejado allí, como fantasmas. Solo usted puede luchar en la batalla diaria contra estos ecos dolorosos. Crea que con el tiempo, esos ecos se volverán más silenciosos y su paisaje interior volverá a ser un santuario.

## Análisis separado

A medida que revisa eventos pasados, conversaciones y sentimientos, el método más saludable para que usted emplee es algo llamado análisis "desapegado" o "frío". Esto significa que no está reviviendo las emociones que sintió durante estos momentos, solo está recordando estos momentos y observándolos desde lejos como si le estuvieran sucediendo a alguien más, no a usted. Tomará tiempo y práctica, pero repasar estos eventos de una manera neutral y objetiva, lo ayudará a obtener el aprendizaje que necesita de ellos, sin llevar la carga de las emociones difíciles una vez que se les unen.

Muchas personas usan diarios personales para procesar eventos difíciles, pero en el caso de Abuso Narcisista, la escritura puede despertar esas viejas y dolorosas emociones, enviándolo a períodos de revivir el abuso y experimentar las emociones nuevamente. Hable con su terapeuta para ver las mejores maneras en que puede volver a contar las historias, si es necesario, sin revivir el dolor.

**El resto del mundo no son narcisistas.**

Después de sufrir la impresionante traición y el dolor que conlleva alejarse de las secuelas de una relación abusiva con un narcisista, debe concentrarse en usted mismo, volver a aprender quién es en realidad y recordar cómo hacer las cosas humanas básicas en las que confiaba antes de ser arrastrado al mundo del narcisista.

Sin embargo, cuando termine este período inicial, puede comenzar a mirar al resto del mundo. Obviamente, no es una buena idea apresurarse a entablar nuevas relaciones, pero lo que es más importante, debe evitar creer que solo porque fue herido por un narcisista, todos los demás con los que se encuentra también son narcisistas.

Ahora que sabe qué obervar, puede ver señales de alerta de inmediato, recordando que los primeros 7 encuentros con un narcisista generalmente serán muy agradables. Una vez que comience a ver evidencia de falta de empatía, falta de habilidades para escuchar y signos de grandiosa confianza o arrogancia, puede maniobrar hábilmente lejos de otra situación potencialmente abusiva. La clave aquí es prestar atención. Alguien que tiene un mal día y no debe concentrarse en las aportaciones de otra persona (temporalmente, tal vez su bebé los mantuvo despiertos toda la noche o han estado trabajando en turnos dobles durante una semana) no implica que es un narcisista. Use el conocimiento vital que aprendió de primera mano para determinar mejor quién es y quién no.

## Crea que merece compasión

Este es uno de esos momentos en que "fingirlo" hasta que lo "logre" puede ser útil. Debe salir adelante de la autocrítica y comenzar a practicar la autocompasión. Incluso si no cree que es digno de compasión al principio, si su monólogo interior está lleno de cosas como *eso está bien*, o *eres una buena persona* o *mereces amabilidad*, eventualmente, esto se volverá rutinario y, en vez de sentir que un impostor está leyendo líneas de un guión, creerá que las palabras que repite son verdaderas.

Comprenda que lo que le pasó pudo pasarle a cualquiera. No es la única persona que comete errores o no es la única persona a la que un narcisista puede engañar. Algunas de las personas más fuertes del mundo han caído presas de los mismos depredadores y salen del otro lado para vivir vidas productivas y felices. También usted puede.

Una herramienta poderosa en la sanación post-narcisista es la meditación y el mindfullness. La meditación a menudo tiene mala reputación por ser demasiado complicada, demasiado New Age, tener afiliaciones religiosas y ser algo que las personas con mucho más tiempo en sus manos pueden hacer, no la persona común. Todo esto no podría estar más lejos de la verdad. La meditación es casi universal y se basa en ideas tremendamente simples. Si uno toma una pequeña cantidad de tiempo cada día para sentarse con una buena postura y practicar la respiración profunda y el pensamiento desapegado, uno puede reducir el estrés en el cerebro y en el cuerpo, prolongar la longevidad, combatir la depresión y la ansiedad e incluso mejorar la función cognitiva con el tiempo. . Eso es todo al respecto.

Una de las cosas que hará un practicante de meditación es algo llamado "pensamiento desapegado". Los pensamientos invadirán el espacio de la mente, es inevitable incluso para un meditador experimentado. Sin embargo, durante la meditación, en lugar de permitir que ese pensamiento invasor lo lleve a una discusión o examen exhaustivo, simplemente marque ese pensamiento como lo que es y deje que se aleje. Un recuerdo de *cuando fuimos al restaurante, cuando arrojó un plato contra la pared, la noche en que conduje hasta la casa de mi hermana y dormí en su sofá.* Reconocer los pensamientos y recuerdos pero nada más. Al igual que el juego de un niño en un viaje en automóvil para describir lo que ven: *pájaro, árbol, tren, casa,* simplemente está marcando los pensamientos y permitiéndoles caer, en el estado tranquilo y sin interrupciones del mindfullness.

**Cuando el desprendimiento completo no es una opción**

Desafortunadamente, muchos sobrevivientes de una relación narcisista deben mantenerse en contacto con su abusador debido a los niños. Esta es quizás la cosa más cruel de todas, y su ex pareja narcisista intentará todo lo que esté en su poder para usar esta relación necesaria para lastimarlo. Lo mejor que puede hacer por usted y por los niños es no engancharse y no tomar represalias. Con el tiempo, otros verán la verdad de lo que es: que su ex está mentalmente enfermo y que no tiene la culpa de su infelicidad. Sin embargo, si se engancha con su ex y sigue luchando, puede ser imposible para alguien determinar dónde termina su ex y dónde comienza usted; ambos pueden parecer inestables. No solo eso, sino que engancharse con un narcisista es como arrojar gasolina al fuego. Solo incitará una mayor reacción y dolor sobre usted mismo.

Uno de los métodos de reacción que más enfurece a un narcisista es una reacción completamente no emocional. El trato silencioso es una respuesta hiriente, y eso no es de lo que estamos hablando aquí. Pero cuando sea su turno de hablar, ya sea por un correo electrónico que tenga que ver con los niños, o una reunión con sus abogados de divorcio, hágalo de manera neutral, sin lenguaje hiriente o tonos acusatorios. Su ex puede alcanzar niveles más altos de ira, pero podrá resistirlo sin dañar su psique o reputación.

## Lento y Seguro (gana la carrera)

Puede haber muchos días en los que deseará poder simplemente subirse a su automóvil y poner miles de millas entre usted y su antiguo abusador, pero incluso eso no lograría la curación que necesitará. Su narcisista aún trataría de buscarlo, incluso si se mudara al otro lado del mundo.

Las batallas que enfrente se quedarán allí frente a usted, así como dentro de su propia mente y corazón. Es posible que tenga que pelear estas batallas frente a su abusador si se junta con usted. Debido a la dificultad de esto, debe tomar las cosas con calma y tener paciencia consigo mismo de que con el tiempo, las cosas estarán bien, usted estará bien.

No tenga miedo de comunicarse con su red de soporte de confianza si siente que está a punto de retroceder. El viaje de la sanación nunca tiene inclinaciones perfectas; hay picos y valles en el camino. No se asocie con nadie que lo avergüence por seguir sintiendo dolor y pérdida un mes, un año, cinco años después. Todos lloran y sanan de manera diferente, y las emociones nunca deberían ser fuentes de vergüenza.

Piense en lo que quiere en su vida y piense en dónde puede encontrarlo hoy, ahora. Piense en las personas que personifican estas cosas. Rodéese de la mayor positividad, gentileza, perdón y compasión que pueda. Estas son las mejores partes del ser humano, y son reales, existen y no son debilidades, los más grandes héroes del mundo las practican. Hay innumerables dichos zen sobre cómo una corriente que fluye suavemente puede tallar la montaña más alta y formidable, y cómo el viento no puede romper el árbol que puede doblarse con el viento.

La prueba de esto es que está aquí, de pie ahora, y aún no está roto, no completamente. Ha resistido las tormentas constantes para salir del otro lado, aún con la esperanza de una vida feliz. No se regañe por tener esta esperanza. Es la mayor señal de que es una buena persona y de que es lo suficientemente fuerte como para creer en usted mismo y en el bien del mundo.

Es un héroe por elegir estos aspectos de la vida y alejarse de la crueldad y el narcisismo.

# Conclusión

Gracias por llegar hasta el final del *Narcisismo: comprender el trastorno de la personalidad narcisista*. Espero que haya sido informativo y capaz de proporcionarle todas las herramientas que necesita para estar seguro frente al narcisismo y liberarse de cualquier situación tóxica en la que usted o un ser querido puedan encontrarse.

Ya sea que su narcisista sea quien haya roto repentinamente la relación, o haya decidido tomar los pasos necesarios para liberarse y comenzar a sanar del abuso emocional, lo más importante es obtener ayuda ahora y comenzar a reconstruir su red de apoyo. Quizás se has alejado de todos los que conocía porque su pareja tóxica sistemáticamente hizo lo imposible para mantener estrechos lazos con nadie más que con ellos mismos. Ahora es el momento de comunicarse, explicar a las personas de su confianza (y que no son también amigos del narcisista) lo que sucedió, y dar el salto de fe necesario para creer que no lo culparán por su abuso. Los siguientes momentos pueden ser aterradores, pero recuerda: fue lo suficientemente fuerte como para sobrevivir a esto, y es lo suficientemente fuerte como para mantenerse libre. No se permita volver al narcisista, pase lo que pase. La regla de no contacto es muy importante porque la mayoría de los narcisistas tratarán de recuperarlo con los mismos métodos que emplearon para cortejarlo: encanto, adulación, atención, afecto, cuidado. Recuerde que todas estas son fachadas, aprendidas al observar a las personas sanas expresarse amor entre sí y que el narcisista es incapaz de tales cosas porque en el fondo no tiene amor propio, solo ira, solo desprecio, solo un deseo de hacer que los demás se doblegen a sus deseos

La otra posibilidad es que su narcisista intente forzarlo para que regrese con él. Pueden amenazarlo con un chantaje emocional o amenazar a su familia o sus hijos, ¡incluso a su mascota! Si tiene participaciones financieras mutuas, pueden amenazar con demandarlo por todo el asunto o arrastrarlo a la corte hasta que sea demasiado miserable para pelear más. Además de una red de apoyo y un buen terapeuta, encontrar asesoría legal podría ser crucial en este momento. Para las mujeres víctimas de abuso, muchas agencias ayudan con asistencia legal pro bono para que pueda recuperarse y comenzar una nueva vida.

Ahora hay muchos grupos de apoyo para las víctimas de Abuso Narcisista. Hombres, mujeres y niños de padres narcisistas están aprendiendo que los números son fuertes y que ciertamente no están solos. Extienda la mano hasta que encuentre una comunidad que pueda ayudarlo a ver que no estaba "todo en su cabeza", y que sus miedos y experiencias fueron reales, no imaginados. Aprenda cómo otros sobrevivieron a su terrible experiencia y tome notas para el camino por delante. Ninguna víctima debería tener que luchar sola; Hay demasiados recursos disponibles para la víctima del abuso como para permitir que eso suceda.

Es posible que tenga que hacer sacrificios en el camino hacia la sanación. Muchas veces, las víctimas de los narcisistas se van impulsivamente, aprovechando la oportunidad cuando su fuerza es la más alta o cuando su pareja no está en casa. Puede tener pertenencias que dejó atrás. Si debe recuperarlos, traiga un amigo o varios amigos. Uno puede hablar por usted, otro puede guiarlo a través de la experiencia, bloqueando efectivamente las palabras mordaces del narcisista; Aún así, otro puede registrar el momento para futuras pruebas. No se involucre con el narcisista usted mismo; sería mejor considerar esas pertenencias olvidadas como una pérdida que arriesgarse a ser forzado a regresar a la relación.

Crea que, como tantos otros antes que usted, tiene la fuerza para liberarse del Abuso Narcisista. Simplemente tomarse el tiempo para aprender sobre el narcisismo y las formas en que afecta a todos a su alrededor fue un paso importante en su viaje, o en el viaje de un ser querido que está sufriendo. Gracias por preocuparse lo suficiente como para querer algo mejor para usted y su familia.

CPSIA information can be obtained
at www.ICGtesting.com
Printed in the USA
BVHW040953060321
601818BV00012B/1920